Emer McCourt is an Irish write[...]
Previously she was an actress, [...]
Loach's *Riff Raff*, before becom[...]
Human Traffic. *Elvis, Jesus and* [...]
Pendleton May First Book Award and the YoungMinds Book
Award.

'Funny and touching' *The Times*

'Beguiling, professional and promising' *Dubliner*

'McCourt writes with a lively style, seeing the world through
the clear eyes of a child . . . an engaging debut' *Time Out*

'A bittersweet debut novel from the actress who proves she's as
comfortable wielding a pen as she is treading the boards' *OK*

'Touching and funny, *Elvis, Jesus and Me* marks McCourt as a
writer to watch' *Image*

'If anyone has formed an Emer McCourt fan club, then please
let me know. I'll join straight away after enjoying her debut as
a novelist' *What's On London*

ELVIS, JESUS AND ME

EMER McCOURT

Virago

A *Virago* Book

First published by Virago Press 2004
This edition published by Virago Press in June 2005

Copyright © Emer McCourt 2004

The moral right of the author has been asserted.

A CIP catalogue record for this book
is available from the British Library

ISBN 1 84408 122 2

Typeset in Optima by M Rules
Printed in Great Britain by
Clays Ltd, St Ives plc

Virago Press
An imprint of
Time Warner Book Group UK
Brettenham House
Lancaster Place
London WC2E 7EN

www.virago.co.uk

To my mother, Agnes

Acknowledgements

I would like to thank the following people:

Thanks to my agent David Godwin and my editor Lennie Goodings. Thanks also to Mary Aver. To Alex West for being fabulous and to Lisa Helmanis and Gena Dry for being the best lucky stars. Thank you to all the gang in Dublin for their support . . . Peter Ward, Vanessa Barcroft, Pat McGonagle, Oonagh Foy, Mick Kennedy, Colin MacEochaidh, Ruth and Paddy Sands and Sharon and Hakan Hjalmers . . . party on! Thanks also to Fiona and Uwe Gratzer and Ciaran and Margaret McCourt for lots. A big thanks to Simon Ryan at Ryan Art and to Margaret Daly. Thanks also to Sister Maria Cox and to Anne Jones for their information, to the Quinn brothers for their knowledge on farming and to Hugh Largey and family.

And finally a very special thanks to my beloved Jona, Ella and Hugo.

Chapter One

I hate beginnings, which is sort of awkward because there are a lot of them about: First Holy Communion; New Year's Day; 'ready, steady, go', that sort of thing. That's why I don't like stories as a rule. Don't get me wrong, I love books but stories that start with 'Once upon a time' – I get depressed when I hear those words. I'd rather someone tell me something that happened, like in life, where it just takes off in the middle of stuff, like a party or a funeral when everything is in full flow. Given half a chance, I prefer to mix things up a bit: back to front; upside down; inside out. It's topsy-turvy, I know, but that's just the way I am.

Last year on the first day of the Month of Our Lady, the girls in our class decorated statues of the Virgin with daisies and Dana O'Leary plucked 'He loves me; he loves me not' on the petals of her offering. As the final petal fell to the floor at her feet, she glanced across at me, daring me to disagree with the verdict: 'he loves me not'. I almost ran over and kissed her, just to show her how wrong holy flowers can be, but I didn't. That was a real opportunity to mix things up and I missed it because I'd never kissed a girl before and I just wasn't sure where to begin. That depressed me, I can tell you. I borrowed the answer book from the teacher's desk and worked from the answers back to the questions just to prove to myself that inexperience in one field does not mean losing out in another.

Next day, Mick, the school caretaker, clocked me slipping the book into the top drawer before class and, during lunch, he reported me. We all thought Mick was deaf and dumb. I, for one, had never heard him utter a word until that afternoon, when he did a Judas on me in the head teacher's office. Mick must have been edging for a promotion because the following week he was doing break-time watch. We learned pretty quickly that he had eyes and ears on the back of his head and a mouth he knew well how to use. He transformed himself from a mute to *The Bionic Man* overnight. If that's not topsy-turvy I don't know what is. My mum says I have that effect on things because I was born with my legs first but I don't really want to go into that. Some things you know about, like how much brake horse-power a Ferrari has, and some things you don't know anything about no matter how hard you try.

It wasn't just maths. When we had to write up science experiments, I liked to start with the result. I thought it was considerate. Imagine reading the same homework from fifteen kids. There were thirty-two in our class but the girls didn't do science; they got to do knitting instead. I'd have probably liked knitting, if I'd been given half a chance. There's a subject where starting at the beginning or the end makes no difference whatsoever to the middle. I've seen it done: neck bands, sleeve cuffs, front and back panels, unravelled then stitched and pearled into new hats and jumpers quicker than you could say 'Beam me up Scotty'. That sort of thinking is right up my street.

Now, take my sister, Ger; she hates endings. She makes stuff all the time, like a rag rug or a *Blue Peter* robot, and stops when she's just one stupid piece from the end. Mum says she's like that because she was a month overdue. My dad told her that if she'd been born into an Indian tribe, they'd have left her on the side of the road for arriving so late. Charming. The way I saw it was, she was just happy where she was and why spoil a good thing until you have to? Clever.

In case you wondered, I'm not beginning this anywhere near the end, or the beginning for that matter, but somewhere smack in the middle because that's the summer that was the beginning of something and the end of something that's still rolling on.

Ger had just turned twelve. There were ten months between us and I wasn't looking forward to leaving eleven behind if her behaviour was anything to go by. If you ask me, she was turning a bit funny. She didn't want a cake or a party this time. She came home after school and just announced,

'It's official, I'm a boy. Mum, you have two sons from now on, isn't that great?'

3

Mum was boiling cloths over the stove and something happened like when someone changes channels during *Doctor Who* in the middle of the Daleks. Like a pause. I don't know. She turned around and had a look on her like a bee had stung her, only she couldn't let out the scream. She spoke with her chest all tight and pushed out like a chicken.

'You can't just turn yourself into a boy.'

Ger went for milk and biscuits, as if she was talking about *The Waltons*. She talked about them a lot.

'I don't want to be a girl, that's all, and I'm not turning *myself* into a boy; the Baby Jesus is helping me.'

'What has the Baby Jesus got to do with it?'

'I'm praying and I know that pretty soon, he'll give me a willy just like Seany.'

'But love, what do you mean? That's crazy talk. You'll never be a boy. Being a girl is great.'

Ger was having none of it.

'Is not. Boys get to have all the fun, and all the money from what I can see.'

She wasn't stupid, my sister, that's for sure.

'They get to fly to the moon, score goals, ride on the back of tractors, and that's just for starters, tell me one girl you'd like to be.'

Mum looked at me as if I was supposed to come up with something but right there and then I couldn't think of one girl I'd like to be apart from, say, the Virgin Mary. She *did* give birth to the Son of God, which was pretty unusual but if I had a choice between being her and being George Best, I know which

4

I'd choose. The way I saw it, the Virgin only did 'the Big Job' once and George Best got to score goals for Northern Ireland over and over again. No competition.

The only other girl I could think of was one I definitely wouldn't like to be. On St Patrick's Day, Ginny Malone sat herself in goals with no knickers on and opened her legs for the world to see all the way to Canada and beyond. Some guys looked; well, you couldn't miss it. Finally I walked right up to her and told her to go home and put some knickers on; that whatever she felt like now, she'd be pretty uncomfortable if Frankie-the-Golden-Shot kicked one of his killer volleys and it landed where the sun don't shine. The next day, when her dad stormed round to our house accusing me of looking at his daughter's 'privates', which is what she told him, all Hell broke loose and my dad whacked me hard. Joe, my best mate, Ginny's brother, was dragged into the whole thing and he had to own up to the truth, so his dad whacked him so hard we didn't play on the same team for over a month. That was all over a girl's stupid fanny. My dad always said, 'Never let women interfere with horses, football and beer.' He laughed at it, like it was a joke, but after all that palaver I knew it wasn't a laughing matter and I pretty much gave up on girls after that. Come to think of it, I wasn't surprised when my sister decided to give up on girls too.

'If Ger wants to be a boy and if the Virgin, the Baby Jesus, the Father, the Son or the Holy Ghost for that matter have any sense at all, they'd tell the Big Man upstairs to sort out a miracle and be snappy about it.'

The entire business about the Holy Trinity was a hell of a conundrum. Mention the lot and cover your options, I say.

I thought Mum would be pleased. She always said that she wanted us to be clear about what we wanted and Ger was pretty definite about this. Instead, I saw that look creeping over her eyes like dropping a stone into a well and waiting, hearing nothing and wondering for days afterwards if it was still falling, as if she was off drowning her thoughts in America or Australia. We knew about those places because Mum's brothers and sisters had emigrated to Canberra and New York. They sent us goodies every Christmas that we couldn't buy in Northern Ireland. Things like chocolate footballs, Kennedy tea towels and clockwork kangaroos. They even sent us stuff we *could* get, like jars of peanut butter. Boy, they must have felt sorry for us living in Northern Ireland when they had sunny beaches and the Empire State Building. I sure did.

'Come on Ger.' I took her by the arm. 'We'll make a cup of tea.'

Mum smiled at me from that falling place and it went through me like pins and needles.

'Two sugars, son.'

'I know, Mum.'

'I'll do the sugars,' Ger chirped.

'OK son.'

Well that was it. I had a new brother, Mum had a new son and Dad, well, he was none the wiser.

Chapter Two

It was May 1973. Reports of shootings and all sorts of carry-on came thick and fast from Belfast and everywhere else, from what I could see. We lived on a council estate in Ballyclough, a few miles from Dunvalley Town, on the border, half a mile from 'no man's land': a strip of land a mile wide that belonged to neither the North nor the South, the British nor the Irish, the Unionists nor the Republicans, the Protestants nor the Catholics, the Devils nor the Saints. When driving across the border along the Dublin road, you passed a British Army barracks at one end and an Irish Customs House at the other. In between was like the Wild West. People who lived there didn't have to pay electricity bills or have television licences because it was a red-tape nightmare that would have needed its own government to straighten out; so the Irish and the British just let them get on with it. The kids probably didn't have to go to school or do homework either. It would have been great to live there, except that the back roads with no names were used for dumping dead bodies with no homes to go to.

'They'll all kill each other before there's peace on this God-forsaken rock and it won't be too soon,' Mum said, every time a body was hauled out of a ditch. She hated killing and shooting, whichever side was getting it, and I don't blame her because whatever you think about politics, a wake is a wake when you're a mother and you can't argue with that.

Our house was on the corner, facing the Green, which wasn't really a green at all. It had been tarmacked over years before but everyone, even the new kids, called it the Green. Mum said it showed you just how stubborn the Irish really were but Dad said it showed they had a lot of imagination. Mum and Dad liked to argue about that sort of thing. Listening to them both would have murdered a saint.

We lived next door to the Murphys who lived next door to the Hughes who lived next door to the Plunketts who lived next door to the McElwees, who lived next door to the Riordans who lived next door to the O'Learys at the top end of our row. I knew all the numbers and who lived where but I'd never stood inside the hallway of a single house. Mum often talked about how charitable I was, the way I was first to volunteer to collect money for starving babies during Lent. I'm not saying that I wasn't happy to raise money for a good cause but that wasn't the real reason I did it. A charity gave me access; a legitimate reason to get a sense of things behind closed doors. Grandad Reilly used to say, 'Get what you want by legitimate means but if that doesn't work, to have no fear and go the long road.' Well, with a clipboard under my arm, I got to stand on everyone's porch with no need to go the long road. When it was collection day and they went to fetch their purses, door after door closed over and wafted the insides of houses into my face like strange flowers. The Carraghers' smelt of chips; the Cunninghams' of Custard Creams; the O'Kanes' of freshly washed jumpers; the Sullivans' of starched collars; the Riordans' of conkers and the McElwees' of shiny shoes. Whenever Mum filled the tank with petrol in the station, Ger would sit with the window open, sniffing the air like it was saving her life. Well, petrol didn't do it for me, but the insides of houses; the whole thing gave me a picture of life that was sweeter than it tasted from where I was standing at the time. It sure was difficult to figure out why our own house smelt of nothing at all.

I don't know who made the 'house rule' but no one ever broke it, which was why the O'Rawe sisters were so weird. They lived down by the garages in the row of houses opposite us and they did quite a few things that were weird. Their father was a long-distance lorry driver and their mother worked in a café for truckers along the border so she wasn't around much either. Everybody whispered about what went on when their parents were home and they whispered even more about what went on when the sisters were home alone. On the outside, their front door looked the same as ours, but you knew full well that stuff went on inside that was as different as you could get.

To the British Army in helicopters, flying overhead on their way to the barracks in Forkmaglin or Dunvalley town, our estate

9

must have looked like a crossword puzzle: all little squares in rows, with hidden meanings and no clues, stuck on to a green page with mountains and bog for boundaries.

Outside the rectangle of houses that lined the sides of our Green, the crossword branched out and along in a pattern of squares that spelt home to about forty houses called Cherryview Estate. Then, beyond McNamee's sweet shop at Riordan's corner, it turned into fancier houses that were called Cherryview Lawns. Cherryview Lawns also faced a green, a proper green, that was dotted here and there with trees and bushes that flowered in springtime. Our makeshift football pitch, where we spent most of our free time, was across the road from Cherryview Lawns on one side and ran along the kerb that marked the Top Road, next to Boyle's farm on the other side. When a stray ball landed in the Cherryview Lawns rockery, old Mr Morrissey, who had nothing better to do, would rush out, waving a fist at us as if we were gypsies not good enough to wash his car. Little did he know that his own grandson, who lived with him, often hung around on the edges of our pitch, all wilted and pale like a sick flower, desperate to get a kick of the ball. Some people see only what they want to see and if you ask me, it makes the whole world a crossword puzzle without any clues. My Grandad Reilly, who didn't go to school much when he was a boy, used to say that he always believed if he worked his hands and his head, he'd get by well enough, even though the land was bad around where he lived. Now, that's all very well if you're a farmer but what if you're not. It left me thinking that I needed different clues than

Grandad Reilly and maybe even Mum and Dad, if I was ever going to get by and make sense of the blank spaces all around me.

Basically, I don't know too much about the Troubles. They are everywhere and nowhere all at the same time, sort of like the Holy Trinity. I mean, if you tried to make head or tail of it, you'd end up inside Armagh Hospital with your brains so fried they'd feed you to the fish. From what I can see, everyone has got a different story about what is going on and who is the cause of it. Our Head Teacher, Mr Murphy, curses the English and says Ireland would be Heaven itself if they hadn't held Michael Collins up by his short and curlies and made him sign the treaty. Granny Reilly says that you can never trust a Protestant because they killed off all the priests during the reign of 'that heathen, King Henry the Eighth.' She says, if that's not proof that all Protestants are going to Hell, then nothing is. My Uncle Pat says that the English have been trying to murder the Irish for over seven hundred years and the Irish are still fighting them off. Then there's old Christie Cole. Nobody I know talks to Christie Cole but Christie Cole talks to everyone. From the moment you meet him to the moment you leave him, he's always saying something about the news, or the weather, or the price of cattle, or the state of farming. Granny says if he stopped for breath he might just drop dead of fright.

Whenever Ger and I stayed over at Granny Reilly's, we would visit Christie because he always had Jaffa Cakes and Milk Tray in his tin. Besides, he couldn't visit too many people on account of his amputation after a JCB fell on his leg years ago. Most people needed two legs to get by in life but from what I could see, he seemed happy enough with just the one. He read books and listened to history programmes on the radio and Mum said, if I had any questions about anything, I was to ask Christie Cole next time we were down for tea. He says that as far back as the days of Cuchulainn, the Irish have been killing the Irish and he reckons that if you put two Irishmen on an acre of land with a rock in the middle, they will soon be spilling blood over who owned the 'good-for-nothing stone that couldn't house a blade of grass'. Curse the English, the Irish, the Protestants or King Henry; it's all Latin to me.

Last Easter we went to Donegal and in the Mount Beag Hotel on Easter Sunday, I met my first ever Protestant, Willy Black. He was ten years old and had a bag of marbles as big as Daniel O'Connell's brain and he knew how to play them better than any Catholic. We were messing about on the stairs and soon we got talking. When he told me he was a Protestant, he must have seen the look on my face because he said I could touch his hands just to prove that he was human.

When our cousins came home from abroad, they wanted to know what it was like living with the Troubles. I didn't really know what to say, I mean, compared to a life sailing and surfing in Sydney Harbour, I guess it was pretty hairy but it wasn't exactly West Belfast where the Shankhill Butchers chopped up Catholics with meat cleavers. On Easter Sunday, we told them about the day when everyone in school had to sit in the canteen until midnight because there was a dead body in the ditch up the road and an incendiary device in the Customs House down the road, so no one could get in or out, until everything was cleared up. My cousin Michael made notes for his essay on 'My Easter Holidays in Ireland'. Sometimes, they would stay over with us and we had to give them the drill about running back home when the soldiers landed their helicopters in the back-fields or when they hung about the playground with loaded rifles. They seemed really impressed with the shootings and bomb scares but personally, I thought it was much more scary to live in a place where you could be killed by a poisonous snake while playing football in your own front garden.

I remember asking Mum if murdered soldiers went to Heaven and she just looked at me funny, like I'd asked her if I could donate my pocket money to the Devil himself. Soldiers were everywhere but we were not supposed to see them, talk to them or talk about them. It was hard sometimes, especially if you came across a sniper lying in the grass when you were messing about in the fields. One evening, last September, on my way back from collecting conkers down at Cully's Castle, I almost fell over one, lying low in the ditch as I was coming home. These two dark holes for eyes shot a gaze at me that would have frozen a lake. I stopped dead in my tracks and stared straight back at him. I'd never seen a sniper so close before, so I took my time, walking around him, studying him like an explorer who'd just come across unknown species.

'Have you ever killed anyone?' I really wanted to know. He looked right through me like I wasn't there. I suppose you have to see people that way if you've got a loaded gun in your hand and you intend to use it. He looked about sixteen or so and I figured he was hungry. 'Do you want some food?' He didn't say anything but I ran home and made him some peanut butter sandwiches. When I returned he was gone; the grass was warm where he'd lain and I left the sandwiches wrapped in tin foil, in case he came back. I went home feeling confused between what Father Cunningham preached in the Gospel and what Mum said about never talking to soldiers. I knew about the parable of the Great Supper, where Jesus said to feed the poor, the maimed, the lame and the blind. I knew that the soldier wasn't exactly any of those things but somehow those black holes where his eyes should have been, made me think he was all of those things at once.

I am so pathetic, I swear, that I even envied Marty Rice and his little brother Bernie who spent every summer with their grandparents next door to us just to get away from Anderson's Town in West Belfast. We saw on the news what they saw on their doorstep and it made them hard and special and dangerous to know. Believe me, if our estate was a holiday camp, they must have had it bad. Apart from our Grandstand Cup Final football match, hearing their stories of riots, plastic bullets, shootings and explosions was pretty much the highlight of last summer. It was as good as having a personal news reporter living in your own back garden. Last July, on the weekend they arrived, a gang of us sat by candlelight in our coal shed and Marty took out a real plastic bullet that he'd found outside his house the week before. We handed it round, holding it with as much awe as we'd have held The Bleeding Glove of Saint Padre Pio. Granny Reilly told us about a wake she attended where a stranger appeared from nowhere and placed a leather glove across the dead man's heart. She said that it was a visitation from the ghost of Padre Pio himself, because when he gently pressed the leather palm, blood from the stigmata dripped down onto the body and the man's eyes fluttered before his soul departed for heaven. Holding that plastic bullet, you felt the same way; something strange and mysterious was taking place yet you knew if you squeezed hard enough, the blood might just seep through.

We sat there, listening to the Rice's crazy stories, knowing that we couldn't repeat a word to anyone, in case Marty Rice got wind of it and called us a grass. We knew that where he came from, people were shot for being a grass and no one was prepared to take the risk that he wasn't the one doing the shooting.

So, while politics was everywhere, it was nowhere, or it was somewhere scurrying about beneath the surface, like a rat darting through Granny Reilly's grain store, that no one could quite get a hold of. Until that summer, I wasn't really aware that our own house was just another barleycorn, rolling down the dryer, with the crushers already hovering outside the door.

Chapter Three

Ger was lying awake in the top bunk with her head propped
against the wall between a poster of Elvis on her right and one
of Neil Armstrong on her left. All three of them faced a picture
of the Sacred Heart of Jesus that shone down on us from above
the fireplace. Ger said that if Jesus ever got depressed about the
sinners in the world, he could glance across at her two heroes
and know that the human race was worthy of redemption after
all. Meanwhile, I was lying in the bottom bunk, looking across
at the crown of thorns, wondering why Jesus bothered to die on
the Cross for all our sins, when the only thing my sister wanted
was to become a boy. If you ask me, he didn't seem impressed
at all with her decision. To tell the truth, I didn't know what to
make of it either. I mean, Ger often got notions that didn't last.
For example, last summer, she decided to build a module of the
Apollo 11 spacecraft, in the coal shed. For days, she wrapped
tin foil around used toilet rolls, egg cartons, cardboard boxes

and Fairy Liquid bottles to construct the command module. She even built a small circuit board that set off coloured lights around the computer console. Like I said, Ger loved to start things rather than finish them and just as she was about to attach the final heat shields and launch herself into another orbit, she left it standing in the corner, a gangly tin scarecrow without a heart or a brain. It was still out there; another half-finished construction to remind me that Ger was as inside out as I was upside down.

'Ger?'

'Yeah?'

'When you have a willy, you'll be able to stand up to pee.'

'Seany?'

'Yeah?'

'Go to sleep.'

'Dad's not home yet.'

'I know. Go to sleep.'

Dad wasn't back from work and his tea was all burnt in the oven like a lump of coal. Mum said that if he wasn't back in time to eat it hot that she'd be damned if she was going to keep it warm, so she left it out on the front porch to cool down. Grown-ups have a funny way of making sense sometimes but Dad got the message. It's funny too just how touchy they can be over things that really don't matter much. I mean, that night Dad wrecked the house, all over a plate of burnt lamb stew. If he'd only stopped for a chicken chow mein at 'The Golden Dragon' because there's little enough space in my head for spelling words like 'sarcophagus' and 'Tutankhamen', without this other stuff taking up so much space, and I can tell you it takes up space.

Ger was praying out loud. She always prayed out loud. She said that God could read your thoughts but why give him the extra work. She was considerate that way. She once took an injured stray dog home without asking my dad. If you knew my dad, you'd know that was a real act of personal disinterest.

'Dear God, please turn me into a boy tonight. I'll be good forever, I'll never tell lies and I'll give all my pocket money to the starving babies in Africa. Come on, God.'

The key turned in the lock but the bolt jarred on the inside. Seconds later a bomb went off in the hallway. Ger leapt down from the bunk and was on the floor quick as a sniper. I stood behind her at the door. 'No,' she said, 'You stay here.' She looked like she knew what she was doing and besides, my knees were jerking so bad I would have fallen down the stairs.

Her feet wobbled on the top stair. I thought she was going to topple over the edge, just like the chocolate Statue of Liberty Auntie Rosie had sent across from the Big Apple for my birthday. It had a roly-poly base and after engaging it in combat with Action Man, it ended up in smithereens on the bottom stair. At least when we picked up the pieces, they were pretty tasty. Ger didn't look so appetising.

She raised her hand to her mouth and uttered, 'Daddy?' I rushed to see and there he was, lying on the floor, face down, surrounded by lumps of coal that were scattered in every direction across the linoleum floor. The front door was in pieces with bits swinging off the hinges like in a Western and there was a big hole in the window where he'd thrown the steel coal bucket through into the hallway. I'd seen our school after the explosion at the barracks and this was just like it. Dad mumbled and staggered to his feet. Mum was watching from the corner and then he went for her, shaking her like a crazy man. She screamed and he was calling her things in a strange voice like a muffled terrorist on the TV. Before I knew what was happening Ger ran down the stairs, over the coal and bits of glass and started to push him. 'Stop it,' she shouted, 'You leave her alone.'

He laughed. I hated that laugh rolling out over itself like a slinky tumbling down a hole. What was so funny I'd like to know. Ger wasn't laughing, that's for sure. She was so busy huffing and puffing like that wolf in the fairy-tale, I couldn't help thinking of the bit where he blew the house down and ate all the little piggies when suddenly the wheels turned and Dad was leaning over her all serious. His two arms were straining with effort as he tried to topple her over, but she caught the crook of his knee and he fell back on to the floor like a crumpled giant. Ger quickly straddled his chest like a wrestler. She would have looked good in a Big Daddy outfit, with her arms raised to the cheering crowds and I would have happily switched stations to *Marine Boy* or whatever; *The Brady Bunch* would have done just as well. Anything but what was to come.

'You leave her alone,' she shouted again. She obviously couldn't think of anything else to say. Then she started to tremble all over, like she was freezing in a snowstorm, and Dad went all limp, throwing his arms behind him like he was sunbathing in the tropics. Weird.

This time I wished he'd laughed but he smirked. It scared the Hell out of me. I swear, he smirked at Ger and said 'I'll remember this on my deathbed, I will, I'll remember this moment on my deathbed.' And then he cried like a baby. What a bloody nutter, I thought. All that melodrama to freak us out, I mean, now I felt sorry for him. He was going to die one day and this would be on his mind as he lay there all close to Jesus or the Devil and I'd have to remember this moment too, as the smell of whiskey was rising up the stairs to where I was teetering on the edge. It caught my throat and between fits of coughing, I knew that I wanted to be part of the picture too. I saw myself rushing down, all heroic like Zorro, grabbing the damsel, then I remembered that Ger wasn't a damsel anymore and she would probably have punched me, the way she was sizing up Dad. Anyway, I was still scared as Hell and my two feet were nailed to the steps like Jesus in the glass case in our church annexe. Whenever I pass that statue on the way to Holy Communion, Jesus smells of whiskey.

Smells get me every time. People talk about birthday parties they remember by the presents they got and I'm so damned weird, someone will mention a holiday we had in Butlins and I'll remember the smell of the chalet that year, with Mum's rashers bopping in the pan to Tony Blackburn, or later when chlorine melted with sugar, as we sat licking candy floss under the fountain spray. Father John, my dad's brother, teaches in the missions in South Africa. He emigrated in the fifties, before I was born, and he has no sense of smell. Everyone is so shocked about it but I don't see what the big deal is. I can't stand the smell of whiskey, it ruins my day. Every time.

Later that night, Dad was playing his Louis Armstrong records so loud we couldn't sleep. I could tell that Ger was listening beyond the music for a door banging or a raised voice. She tried to pray but her teeth were still chattering, so I asked her if I should pray for the both of us. I'm pathetic, I swear, I should have been a missionary, turning to God, all pious like that. Sad but true. I started to chant the 'Desiderata' aloud; 'Go placidly amidst the noise and haste and remember what peace there may be in silence.' That's as far as I got. The priestly vibe really freaked me out.

'Ger.'

'Emm?'

'You OK?'

'I like this one. All that crazy trumpet, I bet he was a good guy to be able to make a trumpet sing like that.' She did that a lot too. Change the subject when things were too out-there. I respect that, I really do, a man's gotta do what a man's gotta do and in this case women were included too, especially ones that were well on the way to being boys.

'Ger, do you feel any more like a boy than before?'

'I wish I could have landed a punch, that's all.'

That didn't make me feel a whole lot better, I can tell you; I was a boy and I felt like punching Dad as much as I felt like running for President of the United States. Being Kennedy might have been okay if he hadn't been assassinated and that put me well off the whole thing. My Granny Reilly was really into the Kennedys and when they were shot, she cried and had a little funeral out the back where she buried a tea towel with their pictures on it. She said that they were 'fine Irish boys who did their country proud'. Granny Reilly also took an hour blessing everything in her sight when you met her. Before she'd offer you a cup of tea, she'd bless 'the tea cup, the tea pot and the hand that poured it'. She would go on for another half an hour to include 'the doors and windows and the hand that built them', so by the time you got to drinking the tea, it would be so cold you'd have to make another pot. I have to say here and now, that dismissing old people because they've got eccentric ways isn't my style. No. I'm just making the point that it's difficult sometimes to figure out what advice to take from certain people about particular subjects. If I was to have eleven children and raise them on a farm in the fifties when there was no kindness for a God-fearing Catholic from the border to the Irish Sea, Granny Reilly is the first person I would turn to for advice, but when it comes to other things, like politics and the Kennedys in particular, I'd exercise caution.

'I'm glad I'm not a Kennedy,' I said.

'I'm not. Even if he was shot, he'll go down in history as the man who sent us to the moon.' My sister knew everything there was to know about the Apollo missions to the moon. The mobile library visited us every fortnight and Ger gave them a whole lot of paperwork asking for books on the stuff. They had to order them especially from the County Library.

She could name every man that landed on the moon since Neil Armstrong.

'What's so great about that?' I quipped.

'You are kidding!' she said. I have to say that I was kidding but I had to get the smell of Jesus in the glass case out of my mind, so I disagreed to get an argument going.

I knew well that those televised space missions were great because we got to stay up late to watch them with lemonade and a "P . . . P . . . Pick up a Penguin". Normally, this treat was only for *Miss World* and *The Eurovision Song Contest* but there was something different about those Apollo missions. The look on my dad's face when he heard the 'countdown' and 'blast off', or the 'Apollo to Houston' bit. Last December, it was like Christmas had come early. Mum woke us up in the middle of the night and Ger and I sat with Dad, watching the launch of Apollo 17. Dad held us so tight, it was as if we were all taking off. When he did the 'Pbshhhusss' engine noises, we laughed, then he told us how great we were. In fact he told us how great everyone was, from Shakespeare to Byron and right through the ages to President Kennedy. There were those Kennedys again. Dad was a teacher in the local comprehensive and he taught some wild boys from Stonecroft Estate. The O'Connell brothers all passed under his cane and they still all ended up inside for armed robbery or possession of explosives. If he failed at one thing, he sure knew his English and I for one wasn't going to stop him in mid-flow. He even quoted Hamlet, the bit where he tells the players to tell the truth, then he went all bleary-eyed. He tried to hide it by slugging on his Guinness and coughing like it was choking him but I saw his lids brim like a cup. I love the Kennedys because of those rocket-launching, moon-landing nights. To tell the truth, I think if my dad is ever on his deathbed, he'll remember those starry nights too.

'Remember when dad choked back the tears last year during the Apollo 17 launch? It goes right through me.'

There was a pause.

'I don't remember.' But I know different.

Ger was still with my other question. I'll give her that, my sister had a memory like a bush-ranger and if you asked her something she'd answer it, whether it was two minutes or two days later.

'The best bit is the picture of the earth from 300,000 miles away. Once you see that tiny ball floating in space, you know that anything's possible.'

'Even peace?'

'Even peace.'

'Is that why you finally decided to become a boy?' I asked.

'What do you mean?'

'Anything's possible.'

'Not especially, just one of a few reasons.'

Ever since I can remember, Ger wanted to be a boy. It wasn't a big deal, just a low-key thing that was only obvious once in a while, like when she refused to wear a dress to Mum's sister's wedding or when she cut her hair with Dad's razor to look like David Cassidy, two days before her confirmation. Dad was furious. He locked her in the bedroom and told her that she wasn't allowed to be confirmed at all. Ger was really upset because if she didn't do it this year, she'd have to come back and do it next year with my class, which would mean doing RE lessons with me for a whole term. One of the other big differences between myself and Ger was what we thought about God and Jesus and all. I was confused and Ger was definite. I trusted Jesus and Ger liked to test him. I asked questions and Ger looked for answers. When she didn't get them, she just made up her own. Take changing the water into the Blood of Christ for example, she challenged the chaplain who visited during our combined retreat, to prove that the water actually changed into blood. He said that she had to have faith. She said that she'd have faith if he could prove it and so on. Mr Murphy had to step in and call a break. Sharing RE lessons would have been about as painful as wrapping freshly cut barley round my privates and trusting someone like Head-the-Ball Murphy to remove it gently, know what I mean.

'Do you still believe that the Blood of Christ is just sweet red table wine, Ger?'

'Yeah, I guess so. I've seen those labels in the Sanctuary. If Jesus can really perform miracles and change water into wine, why does he let the babies starve in Africa and why doesn't he change me into a boy?' Well, she knew how to floor me too.

Recently the lads decided they didn't want Ger to play football. Adrian, our team captain, announced a few weeks before, when he was picking the Saturday team:

'She's a girl.'

'So?' I said.

25

Everyone looked around.

Joe was dribbling on the sidelines.

'Ger's always been a girl.' He chipped the ball towards Adrian.

'Well, that's why she can't play football any more.' Adrian was ready for it. He trapped it with his right foot, flicked it up on to his knee and cupped it into his hands.

'But Ger's one of our best players . . .' 'But she's a girl' and so it went on like the chicken and egg thing until Ger was left standing on the sidelines practising her keepie-uppie. Now take it from me, she was better than a lot of the lads on the team and as good as most, so pretty soon they hauled her in after an injury but the situation was getting awkward.

Funny too how one person has an idea then everyone has it. It's like those forest fires my auntie told us about in the Australian bush. 'Starts off with a spark then before you know, it's a blaze.' She had a wild accent all Aussie mixed with South Armagh. Both Ger and myself had supported Man United for as long as I can remember and a few days after the incident with Adrian, I said to her 'Why don't you go find your own team, Ger. Man U's my team.' The blaze was spreading and I could feel it, I swear, I could feel the heat burning in my gut. I enjoyed it for a second or two, I have to admit, because Ger choked up. She doesn't often choke up and that day she was oozing pain like a Jimi Hendrix fan. Do you ever notice how certain people, not many, have something behind their eyes? I can't explain what it is exactly but I've always called them: 'the people the wind blows through'. I looked out for them the way Adrian looked out for Renaults or Toyotas on the back road on a rainy Saturday. Later that night, when I stared at my face in the mirror, I saw that the wind wasn't blowing through and in that instant, I made the decision that I'd rather be a firefighter putting out the flames than a lame duck adding fuel, so I went to Ger and told her that I was just kidding. I even gave her a football card of my Man United hero, Dennis Law. Thank God for that because I've seen more people than I care to remember with no wind blowing through and I'd be damned depressed if I was headed that way too.

That Saturday, Ger was on the sidelines again. I mean, she wasn't getting any less of a girl as far as Adrian and the other boys were concerned. The summer holidays were around the corner and all we did was play football. If we baked cakes as much as we played football and I was excluded for being a boy, I would have considered a sex change too. That's how serious it was. It was so serious I didn't like to mention it right now but I guessed that was the main reason for her decision to finally become a boy.

'Seany?'

'Yeah.'

'Will you be my witness?'

'What for?'

'I want to ask Jesus to make me into a boy tonight, and I need a witness.'

'Why?'

'It's his last chance, if he doesn't do it tonight then I'm finished with him.'

'Finished with Jesus?'

'Yep.'

'You might just go to Hell for that.'

'I'll take my chances.'

That was Ger all right and I knew she was as serious as she had ever been. I waited for the break between *Wild Man Blues* and *Willie the Weeper*. 'OK' I whispered as the needle crackled along the groove and off she went. 'Dear Jesus, if you are so great, please change me into a boy. I will be good, I will believe in the "water-into-wine miracle", I will not harbour bad thoughts and like I promised, I will give all my pocket money to the starving babies in Africa; come on Jesus, what difference does it make to you? Please . . . Our Father who art in Heaven, Hallowed be Thy Name, Thy Kingdom come . . .'.

I love the 'Our Father'; the rhythm, the way the words roll into one another, God forgive me but it puts me to sleep every time.

Chapter Four

I thought I was dreaming. Velma from *Scooby Doo* was wrestling with a marshmallow one second then Ger was standing at my head holding her pyjamas open the next.

'I can't bear to look, Seany.'

'What time is it?'

'Armageddon.'

'Wise up.'

'I'm serious. If Jesus hasn't heard me, all hell's breaking loose.'

I didn't have to look. I cupped my hand and gently placed it where the bulge should be.

'No bulge.'

'No bulge?'

'No bulge.'

'Right.' She walked over to the picture of the Sacred Heart of Jesus. Mum had slipped a small card with the words

'*Cleanliness is next to Godliness*' between the glass and the frame. Ger stood on the shelves of books, plucked the card from its place and tore it into shreds as she fell backwards. From beneath a pile of books and silver-coated egg cartons, she looked up at the pitiful face of our all-knowing Lord and she let rip.

Now, there was a man in the land of Uz whose name was Job and that man was blameless and upright and one who feared God and shunned evil. We knew about him from the Bible and the way Satan attacked his health and Job cursed the day he was born and on and on he went pleading and cursing until the end of his days. Well, Ger gave him a run for his money.

I slowly dressed myself, waiting for an opportunity.

'Come on, Ger, we're late for Mass.'

We stole into the kitchen and grabbed a handful of Sugar Puffs and a glass of milk. Through the crack in the door, we could see that Dad had fallen forward in his chair as if he'd been stabbed in the back and we quickly turned and stumbled out over the debris in the hallway, like two criminals leaving the scene of a crime. A black plastic bag was flapping in the breeze where the window had been. I tried to shut the front door but it was swollen at the bolt like a boxer's eye. The needle was scratching its way across the end-groove as I walked through and out into the mist.

The cold air hit me like a razor blade and I pulled my polo-neck around my mouth to ease the sting. It was perfect for blowing smoke-rings and Ger kept herself busy all the way past the line of sleeping houses, through Boyle's Patch and on down past the playground where the swings were so stiff with the cold it was as if they'd been painted on to the field behind. When we reached the old parish hall near Cully's Castle she opened her mouth wide and stretched her cheeks as if to yawn but she pushed her thumb and index finger hard against the aching muscle and let out a low moan like a birthing cow. I didn't look.

'Is Eamo doing early Mass with you this week?'

'He is. If he forgets to ring the bells again, he's out.'

'Sure Father O'Looney's so daft he'd hardly notice.'

'True.'

'I want to ring those bells, Seany.'

'What do you mean?'

'I'm a boy whether Jesus likes it or not and doesn't every boy we know get his turn at serving Mass?'

'Yes, but –'

'No buts.'

'But it's one thing *saying* you're a boy and another *being* a boy. That's going to cause a few problems.'

'Nothing that we can't overcome.'

'*We?*'

'Yes. Eamo will do anything I want, so we just have to arrange it.'

True. Eamo wasn't soft but you'd think he was from the way he doted on my sister. She had helped him out with spelling for a while and I can only guess that something happened to him over a difficult word like 'navigator' or 'caravel' because ever since we did the Explorers, he just followed her home after school like a sick dog. When she turned to look at him, he went so red you could have fried an egg on him. He took to leaving little gifts on her desk during break-time: half-used pots of Oil of Ulay hand-cream, with a ribbon around the lid, or a bottle of Charlie perfume topped up with water. When he got home, one of his sisters probably gave him a good hiding. I guess he knew what it meant to suffer for love, since all he seemed to care about was making an impression on my sister. Little did he know that his big chance was around the corner.

At the last altar-boy meeting, Eamo was told he was on his final warning. His two oldest sisters were doing cabaret in the clubs around the counties and the others were talking of entering the Eurovision Song Contest with some local manager and I can tell you, whatever rhythm they all had, he was lucky enough not to get, because with bombs going off all across the country in any pub or club you cared to mention, better be stone deaf and alive in your bed, even if it meant being expelled from serving Mass. He was put on early-morning mass where the congregation was made up of regulars: old Mrs Hennessy who was almost blind; Mr Morrissey who went to so many services he couldn't tell if he was at Mass, Benediction or the Stations of the Cross, and the widow Mrs Byrne, who stabbed so many of our stray footballs, I was sure she'd never lift her head from praying for forgiveness. There were always a few irregulars and then there was Ger, who came to keep me company on the walk past the army barracks up to the church when I was on the early shift.

'I want to ring those bells, Seany.'

'I thought you'd given up on Jesus.'

'That still leaves the Father and the Holy Ghost and besides, how do you know what everyone who serves Mass believes in?'

She had me there. Seamo McNulty was so quiet about everything, he could have believed in Satan or the British Empire for all I knew.

'I want to ring those bells, Seany.'

She was getting hysterical now.

'That might be difficult, Ger.'

'Not as difficult as it might be if I tell Dad you've been looking through those magazines in the back of his wardrobe.'

We used to sing this old song my dad taught us:

> *I knocked a hole in McCann*
> *For knocking a hole in my can,*
> *McCann knew my can was new,*
> *Was only new a day or two,*
> *So I knocked a hole in McCann*
> *For knocking a hole in my can*

until a hard-man from Stonecroft called Jimmy McCann hit me so hard, I could see stars for a week. Well, that was nothing compared to the punch Ger landed and I knew she could knock me into next week if she wanted to.

'What magazines?' It was a feeble attempt.

'Those magazines.'

'What about them?'

'I'll tell him you were looking at them.'

'Was not.'

'Liar. Saw you.'

'My God!'

'God had nothing to do with it from what I could see.'

'Jesus.'

'Him neither.'

The thought of Jesus watching my sister, watching me, watching those women. It all felt like pure Hell already and I knew it could only get worse if the truth came out. I hated Ger at that moment. I'd have hated anyone who saw me there, red as a splattered berry on tarmac and ripe for the picking too.

The only other thing that had a hold on me in the same way as those magazines was the window display of the Star Bakery on Bridge Street. The sight of those delicate cream fancies and fruit tarts, all lattice strips and strawberry jam oozing round the sides, was enough to make me put my hand in my pocket every day if I'd had the money. Luckily for me, we only went into town once a week. Once a week was all my pocket money could afford. If the truth were known, I'd seen those magazines more than once a week and was likely to see them more than once a week again. One after another, those glossy pages transported me to uncharted waters like a dream. I knew all about Henry the Navigator and his perilous trips to discover new lands. I can tell you, if he had discovered the treasures I discovered in my dad's wardrobe, he would never have moved from Portugal to discover Madeira or the Azores; he'd be there still, at the end of the earth, flicking those pages. For Heaven itself was there and why would anyone move from Heaven except to go to Hell itself?

Eamo agreed to hide himself in Father O'Looney's tool shed, next to the church, but we locked him in, before he could change his mind; then we rushed to the vestry to commit our sins. It wasn't long before Ger was standing dressed in the surplice and cassock, grinning from ear to ear like a Holy Saint who had died and gone to Heaven. She got to work like a true professional: the palate, the cruet, the candles and the bells, all beautifully laid out. She had seen me go through the ritual so many times, it was second nature to her. When Father O'Looney shuffled in, he muttered something about the bells without lifting his eyes to check who was listening, which was just as well because Ger was a far prettier sight than Eamo ever was in an altar-boy's uniform.

During the service, I watched Ger from across the altar. She was in her element, as she piously carried the water and wine to the altar and rang the bells with the precision of an angel. By the time Father O'Looney was giving the final blessing, I thought Jimmy Saville was going to walk down the aisle and present Ger with a 'Jim'll Fix It' badge.

As usual, when the service ended, Father O'Looney folded and pleated his robes and then mumbled his way back to the parish house for tea and toast. After she had snuffed out the candles next to the tabernacle and hung up her surplice, Ger thanked me and told me that it was the best day of her life. I wish she hadn't said that because it soon turned into the worst day of mine.

We left the vestry and made our way across the grass to the tool shed. As we unlocked the door, we heard the groans and whimpers of a dying animal from deep inside the shed. I thought of Grandad Reilly, as he watched television by the fire, rolling his fingers through the rosary, moaning when he reached the end of a decade, as if someone had punched him in the gut and left him to die. When we eased the door open, we saw Eamo, hunched behind the lawnmower, eyes wild as if he'd seen a ghost, limbs all jerking like a mad cow. For the first time I noticed just how skinny he was, all bones and freckles, staring up at some God-forsaken vision hovering above his head. Ger rushed to him but he huddled away from her and backwards into the garden furniture, making a racket as he kicked a can of turpentine across the floor. He was flying through the Act of Contrition like he was speeding his way to Hell with no priest to administer the last rites. I couldn't open my mouth, I just stood there gawping like an idiot.

'What's wrong, Eamo?'

'Oh my God, I am heartily sorry for all my sins . . .'

'Eamo?' Ger was shaking him now.

'And with your help I will not sin again.'

'*Eamo?*'

We looked up to where his haunted eyes were fixed like nails and saw the face of St Anthony smiling down at us. I'd only ever been inside the chaplain's residence once and I recognised the statue from the hallway, where one evening I'd sat waiting for his housekeeper to return with a glass of water for Mrs Hennessy who'd fainted during the Stations of the Cross. The statue looked down on me then and I recalled wondering how such a nice-looking man could ask anyone to amputate their own foot for little more than a harmless white lie. The statue must have fallen on to the hard tiled floor in the chaplain's hallway because the one that was staring back at us in the tool shed was changed beyond recognition. The right arm that held the Baby Jesus was missing and there was a hole where the nose had been. It looked more like the face of George Foreman after the *Rumble in the Jungle* than a Holy Saint.

'It's just a statue, Eamo.'

'Oh my God, I am heartily sorry for all my sins' and he was off again.

'I'll get help,' I panicked.

'And get us all murdered? There's only one thing for it.'

Ger always had a plan and right now I was glad of it because Eamo was stuck in something beyond my reach.

She rummaged in her satchel then whipped out a bottle. There it was, the sweet red table wine that turned into the Blood of Christ resting in Ger's hands like an offering.

'A swig of this and he'll soon come round to his senses.'

Ger was already twisting the cap off and besides, Granny Reilly always swore by a drop of the drink for whatever ailed you, so I let the whole thing go.

She reached for a funnel next to the toolbox and told me to put it into Eamo's mouth. Eamo was gentle and cowering now, so I could easily slip the end of the funnel between his lips. Then she proceeded to pour the Blood of Christ down the flute as easily as if she was pouring diesel into a tractor. We stopped halfway and Eamo was still spluttering on about his sins so she just nodded to me and we put the funnel back until we had drained the last drop from the holy bottle. It would later end up, smashed to smithereens on the railway track, beneath a carriage of the eight-thirty express train from Belfast to Dublin.

Ger wiped Eamo's mouth with her sleeve and looked up at the statue.

'God forgive us, but we'd rather this than our dad murder the both of us and Eamo for good measure.'

I hadn't thought of it like that and suddenly I felt relieved. We were saving lives even if it meant blaspheming the Holy Sacrament, so I reckoned that Jesus would forgive us even if St Anthony would ask for an amputation he wasn't going to get.

We were watching Eamo's face as closely as the team of experts at mission control in Houston watching the touchdown of Apollo 17 and we breathed a sigh of relief when Eamo turned and grinned.

'I love you, Ger.'

'Quick, we have to get him out of here.'

'Get up, Eamo . . . Eamo, get up, we have to move.'

He stood up and fell straight back down with a clatter that would have wakened the dead in the graveyard behind the church. We quickly dragged him out of the shed, his armpits slung across each of our shoulders and his feet dangling through mounds of raked grass, leaving behind a trail you wouldn't have to be the SAS to follow.

'Lanky bugger.'

'You bet.'

'I love you, Ger.'

'Shut up, Eamo.'

'But I love you.'

'Shut up, you're giving me an earache.'

We hauled him across a ditch and down to the railway line. Ger ran across and wedged the bottle firmly between the tracks. We headed across the field and away as we heard the express slicing its way to Dublin behind us.

'That statue, it just changed in front of my eyes.'

'Shut up, will ya.'

'It just changed.'

'What do you mean? It must have already been like that.'

'No, the face. I sat there staring and it just changed into the face of the Devil in front of my very eyes.'

'Thank God for that. I thought you were going to say the bloody thing moved, then we'd really be in trouble.'

'Stop joking, Ger, this sounds serious.'

'It'll be serious all right if we don't drag this lump of a sinner somewhere out of sight.'

We knew of a cottage about half a mile from the church across the fields where Kilane Road meandered off the main road and away to nowhere in particular. Mad Tom Flanagan lived there and sometimes he didn't. He kept himself to himself, so no one knew when he left or where he went to but

I heard once that he had family in the South and that explained it. He had the tastiest gooseberry and blackberry bushes for miles around and his apples, every autumn, falling ripe and delicious were a feast for the worms if a gang of us didn't show up to fill our buckets. One of us would scale the tar-lined wall, give the all-clear, then one by one we'd scramble up and drop down into his garden like the Brits melting out of a helicopter into the undergrowth. Sometimes, he would sit back from his window waiting for us and emerge from nowhere, waving a pitchfork, all round head and crooked teeth, scaring the living daylights out of us as we scarpered out through any crevice we could find.

Right now we had nowhere else to go. It wasn't the season for fruit but if Mad Tom was down south then we'd be safe for the day under his apple trees, staring at the clouds and waiting for Eamo to come to his senses.

'There's a map of Ireland.'

'Can't see it.'

'Follow my hand up to that branch, then up to the blue bit in the middle and look left at the patch of small white clouds.'

Sure enough, I caught it just as the North was changing into a ship and heading west across the Atlantic.

Eamo was coming round. He was moaning and rolling his head between his hands.

'Stop staring at the clouds you two,' he groaned.

'There's a ship,' Ger said.

'Where?'

'There.'

'That's not much use. Give me directions.'

'It's gone, now, it's changing into a . . . oh no . . . the Devil himself and it's . . . oh no, it's coming to get us.'

'Very funny, I'm telling you both, I saw it.' Eamo wasn't laughing.

'You bloody nutter, the Devil doesn't live in Father O'Looney's tool shed for a start.'

Ger was right, the chances of that were slim.

'I'm telling you, I was sitting on the peat bags, just looking at the statue, taking it all in, you know, the clothes and the feet, then I stared at the face and it began to change.'

'I stare at things all the time and I don't see the Devil.'

'Same here. That's what freaked me out. Well, apart from seeing the Devil, I figure it's a sign that we're all going to Hell for what we did this morning.'

'Now you listen to me, Eamo,' Ger bolted up on to her hunkers, 'no one's going to Hell, get it? Believe me, you may as well go to Hell, for your life won't be worth living if you breathe this to a living soul.'

'Don't you worry, I'm not telling anyone. For Godsake, Ger, nuns aren't even allowed to serve at Mass. I'm pretty sure we'd all be excommunicated and have to face trial in Rome if anyone found out, never mind what the IRA would do to us for making a mockery of the Catholic Church.'

'Jesus.'

We fell silent. The North, that had changed into the ship and headed way out west, was mingling into one big blanket of cloud.

41

'Look, I saw the Devil's head. Let's just take it as a warning.'

'OK, I can live with that, a warning.' I was keen to end the whole thing.

Eamo might have seen the Devil but he wasn't showing any signs of weakness now.

'You can't serve Mass again, Ger, God knows what would happen.'

'Look, I can tell you both, it felt so good putting on that uniform and doing something useful that I'm not afraid to tell St Peter himself that I'd do it again, just to get a taste of what it's like to be a boy, and there's nothing going to stop me now.'

'You can't be serious, Ger, let's just knock the serving idea on the head.'

'I'll knock it on the head for now but I have a few others up my sleeve.'

'Well, I hope they don't involve Eamo, myself and the altar wine.'

'Not in that order anyhow,' she smiled and nearly elbowed me into next Christmas.

'Fine, a warning, I can live with that.'

Silence again.

'Tell me about this staring thing, Eamo.'

'There's staring and there's staring. I've become an expert.'

'Well, better be good at something.'

'Shut up, Ger. What do you mean?'

'Well, during Mass, if I'm bored I just do this staring thing.'

'Go on.'

'It's brilliant. If you stare for ages at something, say the back of the priest or the mosaic floor or the golden gate to the altar, which is a really good example, and you open your eyes wide like you're mental and don't blink at all, well, in a matter of minutes everything goes black, then the colours come and spots and things.'

'Sounds like being transported in *Star Trek* to another galaxy.'

'Yeah. I think it depends on what you eat for breakfast but if you're lucky you can see all sorts of shapes; once I saw this huge tiger bounding down the aisle towards Mrs Ward.'

'Fantastic, what did you have to eat that morning?'

'Egg yolks.'

'I hate egg yolks.'

'Ah well.'

Mrs Ward was our schoolteacher and she was better suited to her nickname, 'Mrs Hard', for the way she loved to rap our knuckles with the ruler if we forgot our homework. I was enjoying the thought of a tiger leaping towards her when Ger interrupted.

'Eamo, how often do you do this?'

'A lot.'

'Do you think this is why you forget to ring the bells?'

'I suppose so.'

'Well, don't you think you should stop?'

'I suppose so.'

'Difficult?'

'Nope. Now that I know how much you want to be an altar boy, it must be good.'

Silence.

'Thanks, Ger.'

'Takes a woman to show a man . . .'

Mum always joked about that so we laughed but Eamo flashed us a look. I guess he was sensitive to women things, having all those sisters around.

We'd come all this way to discover what was keeping Eamo from his parochial duties. What an achievement for a morning's work: a reformed altar boy, a reformed altar girl, and an encounter with the mysterious. I began to feel like one of Enid Blyton's Famous Five, solving all those problems for the local community.

'Don't you just love the Famous Five?'

'The adventure's not over yet, Julian.'

And, as always, my older sister Ger was right.

Chapter Five

Grandad Reilly used to say that it only takes one bad day to ruin a crop. He also used to say about land: 'The day you buy is the day you sell.' Mum sometimes joked that she didn't take the only useful piece of advice her father ever gave her and look at the trouble she was in now: 'If your father was an acre of land, I couldn't get rid of him for love nor money – the views might look good from the road but stand one foot on the soil and the rocks shift under your feet.' I wasn't sure what she meant but I knew my dad was pretty strange at the best of times. All the kids round our way scratch their heads over the Holy Trinity and all that three-in-one stuff but my dad, well he's about six- or maybe even seven-in-one so I've no big problem with the Father, the Son and the Holy Ghost. Father Cunningham explained it one year by showing us a shamrock leaf with three petals on one stem. It made sense to me anyhow, but have you ever seen a shamrock with six or seven leaves? Not me. I don't envy anyone who doesn't have a dad like mine but I don't envy anyone who has a dad like Johnny Rane's either.

Johnny Rane's dad was always drunk, and I mean always. One night Mrs Rane locked him out and in the morning I could see him from my bedroom window sprawled among her yellow borders. It was September, but Mrs Rane's garden was in full bloom. Mum said she prided herself on having a garden that coloured all year round because living with a man like that would drain the colour out of any woman. I used to think she was speaking from experience but that morning, looking at Mr Rane sprawled among the wash of pink and yellow, with his grey face and crumpled jacket, I could feel something draining out of me too. He lay there, a sight for sore eyes, and I had to glance at her Autumn Mists for relief. Suddenly Mr Rane stirred from the flower-beds. He tried to stand up but he was all folded over in the middle like a broken stem as he hobbled to the back door and went inside. True as God, later that day, he wandered out of the very same door with the very same jacket stuck to his back, headed around the side of the house and out the gate back down to McGinty's, no doubt to start all over again. I didn't wait up to see him come home but the following morning I checked and he wasn't lying in the shrubs. Mrs Rane probably didn't want him draining the colour from her dahlias as well as everything else.

So you see. If Mr Rane was the Holy Trinity, he'd just be one leaf on the shamrock. Simple, no doubt, but I guess a shamrock wouldn't be a shamrock without the other two, which leaves

Mrs Rane in an unfortunate state because not only is she living with a real drunk but a lame shamrock as well. Whichever way you look at it, that can't be lucky. Which brings me back to my dad. I reckon if he was a proper drunk, my mum might have left him, but the worst of it was he only got drastic sometimes and most of the time he was middling and whatever was left, he was sober. And whether he was drastic, middling or sober, my dad could quote poetry or Shakespeare as well as any actor I've seen on telly. But the best of it was, whatever all those words meant, it was like cream to a kitten and Mum's eyes would go all pearly as she curled in towards him and purred: 'Do the one, you know, go on do it', and he would.

> 'I wandered out to the hazel wood because a fire was in
>   my head
> And plucked and peeled a hazel wand and hooked a
>   berry to a thread . . .'

Mum said that if grown men knew how easy it was to get the better of a woman with a piece of poetry, the flower trade would go out of business.

Most other dads I know are one thing and one thing only. After a while that must get pretty boring. Imagine living with Mr Rane, for a start, and then there's Frankie's dad, the champion Irish dancer; Mum called him 'James-the-Heel'. His real name was Jimmy O'Neil but we laughed anyway. That man could move his feet to any reel in the book so fast, you'd think he had wings on his toes. He was always hopping or skipping off to a Feis, a dance class or a concert. You could just imagine him doing a jig to the toilet or a six-hand reel in his sleep. All that talk about concerts, shoes and rosettes would have tried a saint, never mind Mrs O'Neil. My dad, well, he could do a jig if he wanted to but he did a whole lot of other things besides.

One night an old school friend of Dad's came to visit with his wife. We went for a meal to the Ardbeag Hotel as a special treat and between running around the tables, I caught bits of conversation. I could hear Dad's friend laughing and saying every so often, 'Jesus, I've never met anyone to this day and I mean *anyone* as wild as you were, Joe . . . Do you remember . . .' and there was something about a motorcycle and a priest and swinging from a lamp-post, then he'd go back to 'You were a wild man, a *real wild man*, that's for sure'. Mum started to choke on a piece of chicken Maryland. I guess she didn't want to carry that conversation over into the sherry trifle. My dad may have been the wildest student on a motorcycle and God knows what he was doing with a priest up a lamp-post but if ever a contestant got stuck in *The Sale of the Century* quiz show he'd have the answer on the tip of his tongue, no problem. Mum said he'd won that Ford Escort ten times over.

Dad knew a thing or two about a thing or two; he just had a weakness for the drink that seemed to knock the sense out of him whenever it got the better of him. Drastic, middling or sober, there was never a dull moment with my dad. I guess you have to look for the good in whatever situation you find

48

yourself in, or you'd throw yourself straight into the Dunvalley Canal for comfort. No doubt it was frustrating when he went all drastic, especially because you knew he could be middling or sober at the drop of a hat. That particular summer, drastic just took centre stage most of the time. What can you do.

During Dad's binges, Ger did anything to keep herself awake. She would clear out the hot-press, fold sheets or tidy up clothes in the wardrobe, way past midnight. That night, we both busied ourselves, forging Mum's signature by torchlight underneath the blankets. By 1.00 a.m., we were nowhere near the result we needed to get away with bunking a day off school in Mad Tom's orchard. I fell asleep long before dawn but I bolted up when Ger jumped out of the bunk on to the floor. She was standing poised at the door, ready to spring like a frightened deer. Dad was in the hallway no doubt. We heard the keys clunk on to the hall table, followed by the strange rustling sound of a legless ghost dragging its way up the stairs. Ger looked back at me; she didn't know what it was any more than I did. She peeped out through the crack in the door, then pointed to her shoulder and positioned it against the wall; Dad was pushing his shoulder and the entire left-hand side of his body against the wall for support as he bundled himself up the stairs. He was that heavy with drink, I thought the side of the house was going to cave in under the weight of him.

The light-switch clicked in Mum's room. It was usually the starting signal of an engine that just kept going, until it ran out of steam. But this time it was followed by silence. Nothing. Not a sound. Ger gently eased open our bedroom door, so we could hear.

'Jesus, Joe, say something. What happened?'

Nothing.

'Jesus, Joe, you look like you've seen a ghost. What happened?'

Still, nothing.

'Here, let me get you a drink.'

Mum rushed across the landing and down the stairs.

There's crying and there's crying and I never knew it was possible for man, woman or child to cry like this. I'd seen my Uncle Charlie with his arm so far up the backside of a pregnant cow in labour that you half expected his hand to come out the other side; I wasn't surprised at the strange, half-dying sounds that animal made in her efforts to get the troubled life out of her but this was worse than that. Wailing. There's no other word for it. Mum ran up the stairs with a bottle of brandy and if she didn't have a funnel with her, I wish we'd kept the one from Father O'Looney's tool shed, so we could have helped her to rush the drink down him.

'Jesus, Annie.' More wailing.

'Jesus, hold me, Annie' and more wailing.

'Here, get this down you.'

'Jesus, Annie, the bastards tried to shoot me.'

Every bone in my body was hurting. His wails were like daggers shooting through me and I could see Ger was as terrified as I was; they slowly died down and trailed off like the end of a heavy rain. Suddenly, Dad stormed across the

50

landing, switching on the lights, ranting, 'Every light in the house, I want every light in the house on.' He was making his way to us, as we scurried under the covers.

'Not the children, leave the children, Joe.'

'Every light, I said every light.'

He burst in and turned on the light but we were both beneath the covers with our eyes squeezed so tight, we were already seeing stars.

We bolted up in our beds as he leapt down the stairs, stabbing switches in every room and cursing for dear life.

'Come on, you bastards, come on,' he shouted.

'The children, Joe, the children, please.'

'Ger! Seany! Get down here,' he yelled.

'Please, Joe.'

'Down here, now.'

If there had been a sniper in the bed, we wouldn't have been at the bottom of the stairs as fast.

I was hiding behind Ger as we shimmied into the living room. Dad was sitting in his chair holding a bottle of whiskey, shaking so bad, it was spilling over his wrists. His face was as green as a new banana.

'Sit down,' he ordered and pointed to the sofa where Mum was sitting in her nightie.

'Please, Joe, not the children.'

He took a swig of the bottle and held it out like a sergeant major and ordered, 'Drink.'

Nobody moved.

'Drink!' he yelled.

Mum got up.

'Not you. Drink.'

'Joe, please.' Her voice was coming up from that falling place and it went through me like pins and needles.

'Drink,' he ordered.

Ger got up and took the bottle. She returned to the sofa and held it to her lips.

She slugged then spluttered and gulped for air as she passed the bottle to me.

'Joe, please.'

'I said drink.'

I tipped the bottle to my lips, *iasce baithe*; water of life; fire; burning and blinding its way into my gut as I held it out in front of me. For a moment I looked like someone deep in prayer.

'This is a wake, you hear me?' he shouted.

'Drink,' he ordered Mum and she drank again.

'This is a wake, OK? The death of trust. What is it? What is it?' he yelled at Ger.

'A wake.'

'Wrong.'

'The death of trust.'

'What is it, Seany?'

'The death of trust,' it seemed to be the right answer.

'Never you forget it. Trust no one. OK, now off to bed.'

We looked at Mum for a second. 'To bed!' he shouted and we ran out.

At the top of the stairs in the shadows, Ger sat on the step and I sat behind her. We were in a good position to hear what we shouldn't and in a better position to run under the covers if someone was coming.

Between ranting and swigging whiskey, Dad told Mum what had happened. He had been drinking all night in Kennedy's, his local haunt in Dunvalley town. After midnight, he finished up and was walking across the road to his car, when three lads in balaclavas came from behind and ordered him to hand over the car keys. They bundled him into the back and thrust a gun into his ribs, then drove him for a couple of miles, to the gates of the graveyard on the Loughmel road. One of the lads got out and marched him up the gravel at gunpoint. Micky McKee had been a pupil of my dad's from Stonecroft Estate, known among the lads in his class as 'Ginger' on account of his shock of red hair. If his older brothers were anything to go by, there was only one way he was headed but Dad told Mum that he'd always thought the boy was 'exceptionally bright' and had a chance to do something with his life. Mum said she remembered him mentioning it but what Dad hadn't told her at the time, was that he half tormented McKee into learning his grammar and his Shakespeare in the name of opportunity.

It would seem that Micky McKee had his own ideas, regardless of what sense Dad had tried to cane into him. God knows if he was waiting for his revenge or if it was just a chance happening but earlier that night, he was the one who marched my dad up the gravel in Loughmel graveyard, with a loaded gun pointed to his head, threatening to give him 'Six of the best, Devlin, you hear me, six of the best'. He marched Dad to an open grave and ordered him to sit with his legs dangling over the side and to apologise for the humiliation he had suffered during 'his so-called English education'. 'I'll English-educate you, Devlin, what's wrong with a good Irish education? English teacher indeed. Can you quote your Shakespeare now? Can you? Well, go on then.'

Mum often talked about her youngest brother Hughey, who lived in England, and how she admired the way he painted pictures that were so real, you could walk into them. Well, my dad wasn't an English teacher for nothing and he did the same thing with words. As he described everything that happened, I could smell the clay from the open grave and hear McKee's boots on the gravel. I grabbed on to Ger, as McKee ordered Dad to quote some poem from Shakespeare. '"Shall I compare thee to a summer's day? Go on," McKee shouted.'

'"Shall I compare thee to a summer's day? Thou art more lovely and more temperate" and I couldn't remember the next line, Annie, I couldn't remember what came next.'

'It's OK, love, you're OK now.'

'Then I remembered, "Rough winds do shake the darling buds of May . . ."'

'"*Backwards*," he yelled at me, "now say it *backwards*" and he dug the barrel into the back of my neck.' Dad's voice trailed off.

'Jesus, you never asked him to say it backwards, did you, Joe?'

'I did, Annie.' I could hear the shame in his voice. 'He was such a bad git, it was either break him or be broken and if he'd broken me, then there'd have been no hope for him.'

'Or you.'

'I don't know.'

'What would it have mattered, love?'

'I don't know.'

I clung on to Ger and tried to pull her back to the bedroom but she wasn't moving.

'I had to get on my knees in the grave and beg him to forgive me.'

'Jesus, Joe.'

He had the gun pointed at my head. What could I do?'

'Jesus.'

'Look.'

He must have shown her the mark.

'Joe.'

'He dug the barrel so far up my neck, I can still feel it. After God knows how long, the lights of the car pulled up at the gates. I was lucky they arrived when they did because he . . . Jesus, Annie, I don't know. Then one of the other three walked up, threw the car keys at me and told me to get going, that I'd be a dead man if I went to the peelers. McKee shouted after me that he was going to make my life hell, that I should look under the car every time I got into it because he wasn't finished with me yet.'

'I'm sure that's just talk.'

'I checked under that car for a booby trap and I swear to God, I thought I was taking my life in my hands turning the key.'

'You're here now.'

'The car stinks of kerosene and sackcloth; they used it for a gun run across the border.'

'Jesus, Joe.'

Ger was as stiff as a statue. When I looked at her face, the tears were rolling down her cheeks and plopping off her lips like melting snow.

'Come on, Ger.'

'Do you think Dad would care that much about my English if I was a boy?'

'Ger, let's go.'

'He would, wouldn't he?'

I didn't know what to say. When Ger did well in her school-work Dad would just say, 'I'd expect nothing less from you.' She must have thought that he didn't really care but personally I didn't see it that way. Sometimes Dad would go nuts with me and check my spelling and tables. He would pounce without warning, like an RUC spot check and it was torture. During half-term, he sent me up to the bedroom to learn my nine-times tables. When he banged on the floor with the broom, I came down to be tested. He fired questions at me as fast as Blue from the *High Chaparral* shot bullets at empty cans: 'Seven times nine? Four times nine? Twelve times nine?' I suppose I wouldn't have minded if he hadn't taken the bamboo cane down from above the lintel and used it whenever I stumbled over the answer. The more he swiped the more I stumbled and I can tell you, after that lot, I don't think I'll ever care much for nine times anything. Anyway, I don't remember Ger getting the same grilling over her tables or her spelling and I never

56

knew until now that she wished she had. I looked at her and almost told her the truth; that if she was a boy, Dad probably would have given her the same treatment. Then I thought better of it and was about to say, 'Don't be so daft' when the alarm clock in our bedroom erupted. We both jumped out of our skins and leapt across the landing to get into our clothes for school.

We were almost dressed when Mum came in and told us that we wouldn't be going to school.

'Why?'

'Your father has his reasons.'

'Can we go to school tomorrow?'

'We'll just have to wait and see. Now, tie your laces and tidy your room.'

There was such a weight hovering over the house, I would have given up my pocket money for two weeks, just to go to school for the day. Later Mum brought us up boiled eggs with tea and toast.

Ger was staring out the window.

'Are you all right, love?'

She was mumbling something and tapping her finger against the glass.

'Ger?'

Ger raised her voice in concentration, 'Three . . . four . . .'

'She's counting, Mum.'

'Five for silver . . . six for gold . . . seven for a secret never to be told.'

'Magpies,' I said.

'Seven for a secret never to be told.'

Strange.

Ger looked at Mum and Mum looked at Ger and I felt left out of something that we knew nothing about, until much later, when I'd remember that magpie as it flapped its black wings across our window pane on its way to God knows where.

Chapter Six

Two days later, we were walking to school with a sick-note. I was so happy to be out of the house that I wouldn't have cared how much trouble we got into for locking Eamo into Father O'Looney's tool shed. For the past two days, Ger had taken the hump with me. She'd huffled and shuffled on the top bunk like a huge sea-lion, too long out of water. I'd made the big mistake of sneaking up on her as she was hunched in the corner, writing a love-letter to Elvis. I was bored, I guess, I don't know, but I grabbed it from her and she tore after me. I scrambled on to the top bunk and read: 'Dear Elvis, Please will you do a concert in Belfast or possibly Dunvalley town itself? I think that if you did, all the Catholics and Protestants would have to sing along to "A big hunk o' love" . . .' I did a Starsky roll off the bunk on to the floor, with Ger tearing at me as I read on, '. . . that way they'd probably think twice before shooting each other . . .' She ripped the letter from me and I was left holding the corner of the page that read, 'I love you Elvis', signed 'your faithful fan, Ger Devlin'. I fell on to the bed laughing as she stomped up to her bunk. I notched the following thirty-six hours on to my bed-head like a condemned criminal because no matter how much I tried, Ger refused to speak to me. She was as stubborn as a mule when she got into one and I could only blame myself for giving her the option. Dad was asleep most of that time, until last night when some of his cronies came round to play cards. At one o'clock in the morning, we were both lying awake in the dark when Ger finally whispered to me over 'God Bless the Child', that was smoking its way up through the floorboards into our room.

'Why do you think Billie Holliday could sing like that?'

'What do you mean?'

'She sang from her heart, don't you see?'

I wasn't sure I did see.

'How do you know that?'

'Dad told me all about her. She made grown men cry when she opened her mouth.'

'So?'

'What's the point in talking if you can do *that*?'

'Did she never speak then?'

'Well, if she did, she didn't need to.'

I'd heard the record many times but had never heard it. I closed my eyes to listen and something deep inside caught a hold of me and rushed to the top of my throat.

'I guess she must have known a thing or two, if that's what you mean.'

'Yeah.'

'Do you feel the same way about Elvis too?'

'Look, if you have to ask then there's no point in explaining but I will anyway. Elvis is the King, that's all you need to know.'

'But you said before that he sings like an angel.'

'That too.'

'Well, is he angel or king?'

'What's your problem? Angel? King? What's the difference?'

'I don't know how a King would sing, is all.'

'He sings like an angel and he rocks like a King. See why I don't want to speak to you?'

Silence.

'Do you think Elvis is generally better than Jesus?'

'Yes, Elvis is generally better than Jesus.'

'If Jesus had been Elvis, I wonder what religion we would all be now?'

'Rock and Roll.'

'Is that a religion?'

'If I had my way it would be.'

I'm telling you, she had an answer for everything. You'd have needed the rock and roll of The King and the voice of an angel to beat my sister in an argument.

The following morning on the way to school, I broke the silence, just before we hit the main road and left the estate behind.

'Do you think that Ginger McKee really will try to shoot Dad?'

'I suppose anything's possible.'

'What do we do about it?'

'Look, Seany, we can't breathe a word about it to anyone or we are in big trouble, do you understand?'

'But what if he tries to kill us?'

'There are a couple of precautions we can take, that's all.'

'What kind of precautions?'

'We can find out what he looks like for a start. After school we'll check Dad's old school annuals and we'll pin him down. If we see him lurking about, we'll have to do something then.'

'Like what?'

'We'll have to emigrate I suppose.'

'OK.'

I could see that she was worried but there wasn't much else to say about it. Close to the school, Ger stopped at the entrance to Mulligan's timber yard and opened the sick-note. She leaned on a large pile of plaster-board, took Mum's pen out of her pocket and changed 'Geraldine and Seany have been sick for the past *two* days' to 'Geraldine and Seany have been sick for the past *few* days'. She licked the envelope, turned to me triumphantly and beamed, 'Elvis rules!', as we walked on towards the gates.

School was always topsy-turvy for the last week of term. We hadn't missed much apart from concert practice and warm-up heats for sports day. Mrs Ward demoted me from being the youngest brother in *Joseph and the Amazing Technicolor Dreamcoat* to the chorus. I didn't mind because the chorus was on stage for the entire show and from there I could scan the audience for Micky McKee, the way I'd seen Starsky and Hutch scan crowded bar-rooms for baddies. I wasn't sure what exactly to do if I did see his face peering across the heads towards my dad; but I knew well that the first rule of prevention was being caught before the act.

That afternoon after school, Ger and I rushed home. The key was behind the letter-box so we had our milk and biscuits and went straight up to the boxroom to look through Dad's bookshelves. I pulled down last year's year-book but McKee's name wasn't there. Ger was looking through the 1971 book, silently turning the pages, when she gasped. I grabbed the book from her and she grabbed it back. 'It's him.' He was standing in the back row with a smile so broad that he looked more like George Formby with his ukulele than an IRA gun-runner. He had a shock of wiry hair and a face so dotted with freckles that he was as distinctive as the Pope in an Orange Day parade. 'My God, you couldn't miss him if you tried.' Ger rushed next door to our room and came back with her magnifying glass. We stared at his distorted face, taking in every last freckle.

'What's that saying? You know the one, about "enemies"?'

'Know thy enemies?'

'Yeah, I'm sure Jesus said it somewhere in the Bible, so it must be a good thing.'

'He also said to turn the other cheek.'

'If this guy has his way, we'll have no cheek to turn.'

'What does Jesus say about *that*?'

'Know thy enemies.'

'OK.'

'I want to pray that he gets shot or is imprisoned or something, so we don't have to deal with it.'

'Don't be daft, you can't pray for stuff like that.'

I didn't care, I figured it was worth a try. As we knelt there, staring at the face of death, I offered up a quick prayer to St Jude to see to it that McKee came to an early demise: a car crash, a gunshot or even a fall from a great height would do. I started coughing to give me a reason to put my hands to my lips, where I did a quick sign-of-the-Cross, before Ger knew what I was up to. When we heard the car pull up outside, Ger ran to the window and I did another sign-of-the-Cross over my chest, just in case the first one didn't count. Mum was pulling bags of shopping out of the boot, so we shoved 'Ginger-the-Killer' and his schoolmates back onto the shelves between *A Christmas Carol* and *Valley of the Dolls*.

The next day, Dad was home early. His school was winding down for the summer and teachers that were not invigilating were sent home to mark exams. That evening, Ger was in the kitchen with Mum, washing dishes. I was watching *Crackerjack* on TV and Dad was in the dining-room, marking papers. There was a knock at the front door and before I could say 'Crackerjack', Dad answered it. Just as Mum shouted through, 'Tea's ready', there was an almighty bang as Dad slammed the door so hard I almost swallowed my tongue. Dad was screaming orders at us to 'Get down! Get down! Everybody, on to the floor.' We rushed into the hallway and to our disbelief, Dad was rolling along the floor just like Charlie's Angels in a shoot-out, yelling 'Down! Down! On to the floor. Now!' Before I knew it, he took the legs from under Ger and she fell backwards on top of Mum into the vegetable rack. I came peering round the corner as Dad yelled at me to get down and dragged me across the floor and into the kitchen where we all lay face-down between the carrots and the onions.

'What's going on, Joe?' Mum was terrified.

'Not now, Anne, someone just pulled a bloody gun on me.'

Dad started to bundle Ger into the larder, when the letter-box squeaked open and a thin voice crackled along the hallway like a relative on a long-distance call from Australia,

'It's only me, Mr Devlin. It's Smithy. I've come to collect the paper money.'

'Who?' Dad turned to Mum.

'Smithy. The paper boy.'

'Jesus, Mary and Joseph.' Dad stormed out and opened the door. Smithy stood there like a kid who'd just seen a ghost. He was all slanted over to one side from the weight of the bag and at first he looked like he was about to faint into Dad's arms but he quickly straightened himself up when Dad yelled, 'What the hell are you doing, shooting the bloody paper at me like it's a rifle? Who do you think you are, John Wayne?'

'It's the way I deliver the papers, Mr Devlin, they come all rolled-up like this . . .' He pointed to the large plastic bag slung over his shoulder, lined with dozens of tubes.

'Look, son, this is Northern Ireland. People get shot on their doorstep in broad daylight. You should know better than to pull the paper on someone like that.'

'I'm really sorry, Mr Devlin.'

Mum went to the door. 'Are you all right, Smithy?'

'Yeah, thanks Mrs Devlin, you owe for four weeks now.'

'OK. How much is that, son?' and she reached for her bag

that was hanging from the banisters but Dad wasn't finished with him yet.

'Delivery boy, indeed. You've been watching too many Westerns, son.' He touched Mum's arm gently. 'I'm just a bit jumpy, love.' And who would blame him?

Our neighbourhood had two different kinds of people in it. Ones who you would call on when you were doing a sponsored walk and ones you wouldn't call on to save your life. You just knew that some people wanted to be left alone and you didn't have to know why. Last year, on our way back from school, not far from our house, the road was blocked off with red and yellow tape. A small crowd was gathering and as we approached, we could see the RUC Saracens and the army tanks outside the house of a man who no one ever called on, not even for a sponsored fast for starving babies in Africa. We were close enough to see the gunshots that had blasted holes in his front door, there was a pool of blood on the porch outside and an almighty mess of glass splattered across the pathway. I knew this was the scene of something ugly that we shouldn't be looking at but there it was in front of our eyes as sure as the see-saw in the playground behind us. We watched as the RUC milled about and the army stood around with guns, looking through us, into the distance as if we were thin air. The only sound was the crackle of their radios breaking the silence that was upon the place like a funeral parade.

Suddenly, we heard the wafer-thin noise of an ambulance coming through like an ice-cream van on a sunny day. Ger tugged at my arm. 'Shit. He's still in there.' I wanted to watch but Ger pulled harder. 'Let's go.' The crowd dispersed as the ambulance drew closer. Suddenly we both turned and started running, legging it up past the post office to take the long way home.

We ran into the house to tell Mum. I was breathless as I spluttered, 'The man in Number Two, opposite the playground, he's been shot, Mum.'

'Yeah, we just saw the ambulance pull up outside, there was blood everywhere.'

'Yeah, he's still in there, Mum.'

Mum grabbed us both by the hands. 'I don't want either of you down by that playground until I say so. You understand?'

'What did he do for someone to shoot him, Mum?'

'Mr Flanagan was a policeman, that's all you need to know.'

'Why would someone want to be a policeman if they're going to get shot?'

'It doesn't make sense, Ger, sometimes things just don't make sense. Now listen carefully to what I have to say.' She got down on her hunkers and looked at us straight. 'I don't want to hear either of you talking about this again, do you understand?' We both nodded. She pulled us to her tightly and kissed our heads. 'My babies, I'm sorry, I'm so sorry,' she whispered. She was squashing my face against her chest and I opened one eye to look at Ger but she was nestled in so peacefully I thought she'd fallen asleep.

*

Over the weeks, we heard through the grapevine that Mr Flanagan hadn't died but that he would probably be in a wheelchair for the rest of his life. We also heard that his wife had emigrated to an unknown destination and that they wouldn't be coming back to Number Two. I understood enough about the Troubles to know that being a Catholic and a policeman was dangerous. Mum said it was like playing football and constantly scoring own-goals. I'd seen a programme on television with masked voices of RUC men talking about the fear they lived under and the precautions they had to take, like checking their cars for booby traps every time they went for a drive. I'm not saying that's right or fair but at least they knew what they were getting into and here we were, innocently going about our daily lives, suddenly having to worry about being shot on our own doorstep, just because our dad had treated Ginger McKee to six-of-the-best, once too often. Things were making less and less sense to me and I started secretly praying that Dad would emigrate, until this whole Ginger thing died down, just so we could all live in peace for a while.

Chapter Seven

The last day of school: a place somewhere in between the end of something old and the beginning of something new. Right up my street. When it finally arrived, we had a half-day and I and a few of the lads from the class arranged to walk home via Cully's Castle to bridge the gap and start off the summer. But instead of playing hide-and-seek among the ruins, I had a last-minute change of plan and was taking the bus into Dunvalley town, heading to the cathedral for afternoon confession with a visiting missionary.

We usually went to confession on the first Saturday of every month but on that morning, I was struck by a bolt of conscience that hurled me into the arms of the Lord to pray for forgiveness or, worse, to cast an evil demon from my soul. During breakfast, Pete O'Hanlan, one of Dad's teaching buddies, rang and offered him six weeks' work in England. Dad usually did painting and decorating in the summer holidays but he'd never been offered work abroad before. He was to start immediately, painting and decorating a hotel somewhere on the South Coast near Brighton. At first I thought my prayers had been answered but then I thought again. If I really did have the power to make my prayers come true, I was going to be in big trouble over my prayers for the premature death of Micky McKee proved to be equally effective. Whatever I thought about McKee, I did not want to be held responsible for his murder. That would have ruined my summer altogether.

I nervously entered the Cathedral through the side-door, headed straight for the red light over a confessional box near the altar and almost knocked it over, as I fumbled through the heavy curtain on to my knees.

Then the screen sliced through the darkness. I looked up. The light spattered across my face and the bright promise of a new world beyond sin appeared before me. I felt like Captain Kirk entering another time zone on the 'Starship Enterprise'.

'Is there anybody out there?'

The missionary's voice interrupted my flight. I told the priest that it was two weeks since my last confession but that I couldn't wait for another two weeks in case I had a murder on my hands. 'Slow down, my child,' he said in that voice, the voice of piety and godliness that was drawing the poisons out of me like a soothing poultice. I explained how I had prayed to St Jude for his assistance in preventing a potentially violent act and that I was now worried that God was going to make my prayers come true because I had also prayed that my father would emigrate and now he was going to go to England for six weeks. I must have confused him; I'd certainly confused myself. I was about to explain again when the priest said, 'You live in difficult times, my son, and it is important to turn to God in times of frustration and despair and he will understand your need to pray for an end to the shootings and killings you see around you.'

'You don't understand. I wanted God to kill someone for me, and now I want you to stop Him in case I go to Hell for it.' I had to get straight to the point; my bus was leaving in ten minutes.

'Are you telling me that you have prayed for harm to come to another?'

'Yes.'

'Is it your intention to engage in anything other than prayer to realise this mal-intent?'

'No. I told you I wanted God or St Jude to do it and now I want to take it all back. I'm sorry, I'm sorry, Father, forgive me, you have to tell Him to forgive me . . .'

'OK, son. You have seen the error of your ways. The only sin you have committed is one of the misappropriation of the gift of prayer. You have heard it said to love your enemies and bless those who curse you. Blessed are the peacemakers for they shall be called sons of God. Now go and pray for forgiveness for yourself and the person you wish harm . . .'

'But what if he's been killed already?'

'Have no fear, your prayers will have had nothing to do with it. Remember, violent means meet violent ends. In this life you reap what you sow. Say three decades of the rosary, one Our Father and now the Act of Contrition . . .'

As I left the cathedral and skipped down the stone steps, a beam of sunshine hit my eyes and I felt blessed as a rainbow of light burst into colour behind my eyelids. The summer holidays were here, Dad was out of trouble for the time being and my soul was as white as the driven snow.

I got the bus back and had time to stop off at the Green to kick a ball around with some of the lads who were practising penalty kicks for the game tomorrow. I wondered why Ger wasn't in goal or standing on the sidelines showing off her 'keepie-uppie'. When I got home, I soon realised that she was busy gearing herself up for a summer football season neither of us would ever forget. If it was true that you reap what you sow, then this summer was about to turn out as odd as a crop of square potatoes.

As soon as I opened the front door, Ger shouted excitedly down the stairs that she had something to show me. My sister had done some barmy things in her time so I figured nothing would surprise me but what she had in store really took the biscuit. I went upstairs and into the bathroom where Ger was standing by the sink looking curiously pleased with herself. She told me that she had a huge secret to tell me but that I had to swear on my life not to tell anyone. I performed the necessary crossing and spitting and she beamed at me, 'I've done it.'

'Done what?'

'Turned myself into a boy.'

'What do you mean?'

'What do boys have that girls don't have?'

'Brains, good looks . . .' She thumped me. 'Go on . . . say it . . .' She looked down at her crotch area. I was beginning to feel a little uneasy when she turned and lifted a towel from the top of the laundry basket to reveal a selection of sausages lying side by side on one of Mum's dinner plates.

'Sausages,' I observed.

'Exactly. You said it, boys have sausages and girls don't. But not this girl.'

I stared at her in disbelief. 'Oh, my God, what have you done?'

'Don't look at me like that, Seany. I told you I was going to take matters into my own hands.'

'Yes, but you didn't say you were going to take them into your own trousers.'

'Can you see a difference? Can you?'

I looked down at her crotch area and indeed, there was a small bulge where there hadn't been before.

'You're crazy.'

'So would you be if you had to face a summer standing on the sidelines during the Grandstand Cup Finals. Sorry, Seany, but you've got to help me out here.' She flashed me a look and I remembered the magazines in Dad's wardrobe. At the very thought of them, all my white patches were blackening over and I wasn't even two hours out of the confessional box.

'What do you want me to do?'

'First of all tell me which is the best?'

'What do you mean?'

'Well, I've bought a selection: Cookstown's Dependably Delicious; Butcher's Best Pork; Butcher's Chipolatas and black pudding, oh yes and this one . . .'

She carefully placed her hand down her trouser-front and pulled out a withered sausage: '. . . and Cookstown Fried.' Before I could object, she delicately placed an uncooked Cookstown's Dependably Delicious in its place, turned to me and demanded, 'Marks out of ten? Come on, Seany.'

'It looks real, if that's what you mean?'

'OK, and what about this one?' She grabbed the black pudding and placed it inside her trousers.

'Well?'

I had to admit that I'd never seen anything quite like it before.

'Marks out of ten?'

'Ten out of ten for size but zero out of ten for anything else.'

'What about this one?' She went through the lot, parading up and down the room like a contestant in *Miss World*.

'So, which one wins?'

I was very reluctant to admit it, but Cookstown's Dependably Delicious won hands down.

'Thanks for this, Ger, really, I mean thanks a lot.' I was being sarcastic but she was too excited to notice or care.

George Best had been advertising Cookstown's Dependably Delicious on television and you couldn't turn around in the street without someone saying, 'What the man means is Cookstown are the best family sausages.' And here I was now, knowing full well, that if my dream ever came true and I finally got to meet my hero and thank him for dribbling the ball like a God and for being such an inspiration to me, the vision of my sister's sausage-filled crotch would be sure to spoil it. I swear, but she could ruin manure for a dung-beetle without even trying.

Ger was busy tucking in her shirt.

'What now?'

'I'm going to tell everyone that I'm a boy.'

'They won't believe you.'

'I'll show them, won't I, and they'll have to believe me.'

'Jesus, Ger, everyone knows you're a girl.'

'Well, we just have to tell them different.'

'I can't.'

'You can.'

'No one is going to believe that you were a girl yesterday and you are a boy today, it doesn't make sense.'

'I've thought about it and I figured that if we give people a good enough story, they'll believe anything.'

'What do you mean?'

'Well, when we were kids we believed in Santa.'

'I don't get it.'

'Uncle Vincent said Catholics would believe anything.'

'Yeah and Uncle Vincent married a Protestant. Mum says we don't talk about him.'

'That's not the point. I have got a foolproof story that will convince even Adrian that I am really a boy.'

'You might have a good story, Ger, but they still won't believe you.'

'OK, come and see.'

She nodded to me as she gently tugged her Bay City Roller drawstring trousers at the waist. I approached and there it was, nestled into the shadows: a perfectly formed penis that looked even better than the real thing.

'Well,' I said, 'you can't argue with Dependably Delicious.'

'So you'll do it for me?'

'What, you're going to show everyone your sausage?'

'No, I'll agree to show two people, Adrian and Frankie, and that's all I need. So you'll back me up?'

'Do I have a choice?'

'Not really. Plus you know I'm as good a centre forward as anyone you've got.'

'So, when do you plan to do it?'

'I want to play tomorrow, so I figured we should do it this evening before tea.'

Before I could change my mind, we were on the way up to the Green where everyone was gathering for a game. Adrian and Frankie were team captains and as usual they began selecting.

'Flan.'

'Joe.'

'Raff.'

'Malachy.'

'Pud.'

'Liam.'

'Seany.'

'Smithy.'

'Eamo.'

'Desie.'

'Og.'

'Jock.'

'James.'

'Micky T.'

'Paddy.'

'Micky O.'

'Eugene.'

'Ollie.'

'Sloany.'

'Owen.'

'Flynn.'

Ger was left standing with Spud, the fat kid from down by the garages. He always ended up in goals and sometimes Adrian put him in as a goalpost when there were no big boulders around. Spud didn't seem to mind as long as he was involved in the game. Adrian looked at Ger. 'Sorry, Ger, but you're a girl.' She looked him straight in the eye, placed her foot on top of the ball and positioned herself for the performance of a lifetime.

'Well, it's time I told you all, I'm not really a girl, I'm actually a boy, so you're just going to have to let me play.' There was a stunned silence, then someone giggled before Adrian picked up the challenge.

'So, you're actually a boy, Ger? Since when?'

'Well, it's time I told you the truth. But you all have to swear not to tell a living soul.' She looked around and they all nodded that they would swear but she insisted, 'Go on, put your hands over your hearts and swear' and they all did as she asked. I thought to myself, it wasn't Catholics who'd buy anything but my sister who could sell milk to a cow. Once she was satisfied that everyone had crossed their hearts and hoped to die, she continued. 'You know that story in the Bible, the one about the evil King Herod who killed all the male children in Bethlehem and an angel of the Lord appeared to Joseph in a dream saying, "Arise, take the young child Jesus and his mother and flee to Egypt."'

We all nodded, we knew the story well, and Ger continued. 'Well, when I was born, we lived in Belfast and the Unionists issued a secret decree, just like Herod, to kill all the Catholic baby boys, so my mother acted quickly and told everyone, including the priests and other parents, that I was actually a baby girl. It was the only way my mother could save my life. That's the reason there are so many girls in Northern Ireland compared to boys. Anyway, soon afterwards we moved to Dunvalley but they kept me as a girl and now, well, the truth is I'm really a boy.' I nearly fell off my feet. Brilliant. Adrian looked around at the others, who weren't sure what to make of it, and he turned and challenged me.

'Seany?'

'She's telling the truth, Ad.' He looked sceptical but Ger had done such a good job that some of the lads started rooting for her already.

'Seems like she's telling the truth to me,' Flan chipped in and Desie and Og nodded in agreement.

Just as Ger figured, Adrian needed more.

'But being a boy means, you know, you have to have a . . . you know . . .'

'I do have a "you know" . . . Do you want to see?'

'What, you're going to show me?'

'If it's the only thing that will convince you, then what choice do I have?'

Adrian braced himself, nodded towards Frankie and asked, 'Can he see too?'

'OK, I'm just going to show you two and that's it.' She looked to the crowd for approval and they nodded. 'Fair enough,' Joe said. She really had them on her side. Just as she had done with me earlier, she pulled back the drawstring for them to see. 'Well, have a good look.' They both peered over her hands as if they were stealing a glance into a forbidden well and suddenly jumped backwards in fright.

'Jesus!'

'Jesus!' Adrian couldn't take his eyes off Ger. 'She's a boy all right, I've seen it. She's a boy.' He turned to Frankie frantically. 'Frankie?'

'He's right, she's a boy, lads. I've seen it with my own eyes.'

'Well, that's that then.' I clapped my hands together, relieved that the whole thing had passed off so smoothly. 'Let's get back to the game.'

Adrian, usually a great dribbler of the ball, looked shaken and fell over himself a couple of times when Ger came in for a tackle. She really was the man of the match; the ball a magnet at her feet as she controlled it brilliantly down the wing, cut back inside to the penalty spot and slotted it inside the far post, to give our team the winning goal. As we carted her through the goalposts on our shoulders, I reached up and wrapped my hands around her ankles, just in case her Cookstown's Dependably Delicious was jolted out of place and rolled on to someone's head. It would have been as bad as scoring an own-goal, three seconds before the whistle. Ger's life as a boy had a triumphant beginning but as Mum always said, 'Nothing worth having comes easy.' We'd done some daft things before, like holding our hands under a magnifying glass in the midday sun, but that was nothing compared to what Ger was to put herself through in only a matter of days, to welcome herself into a club she would have sold her Man United shirt to join.

Chapter Eight

Grandad Reilly was always old to me. He was a big, heavy man and the way he sat in his chair by the fire, still as a sleeping cow in a field, nothing but the fingers flicking at a string of rosary beads in his hand like a tail at flies, you'd think he was only half-alive, until you moved from the bald patch behind his head to the front and saw into a face that had blue eyes as bright and as clever as a good sow's. He was a man who knew about all breeds of animal from pigs to horses to cattle, so much so that he would know a stray animal on the road and who owned it. Anyway, my mum often looked at me proudly, beaming from ear to ear, saying: 'You're a real Reilly. A barnacle if ever there was one.' Anyone who called my grandad anything, first called him Barnacle Reilly, then they'd curse or praise him: 'An easy man to like and an easy man to dislike, depending on your bent,' so Christie Cole said. When I asked Mum about it, she said that as far as she knew, he'd had the name ever since he was a boy and could harvest good flax on two acres of land that had more rocks on it than soil; and him with nothing but an old swing plough that made both hands bleed just to balance it down through one side of a field. Ever since that time, he got the name 'Barnacle': a thing that could make a living for itself on a piece of rock that was neither good to man nor beast. And the name just stuck.

One Saturday afternoon when we were over visiting, Mum was giving out to me about my homework and Grandad Reilly threw me a wink. When Mum went out to make tea, he told me that he went to school but paid no heed at all to what was going on. His interest was in horses, which was just as well because as he said himself, 'I had nothing to write with nor nothing to write on, neither pen, pencil or book.' Later, when I asked her about it, Mum told me that as far as she knew, he left school at twelve and was ploughing for his father who wasn't in the best of health and who died when he was fifteen years old, leaving him with nothing more than the two acres of land that tore his hands to shreds. Mum said that they knew what hardship was in those days. She told me that when Grandad was a boy, he was so poor that he went to work for a neighbour-man up the road because he had no horse himself and his mother hadn't the price to pay for one. He said proudly 'I helped your man up the road so that with the help of God, I would soon buy a horse down the road.' Another time, when we were down visiting and I asked Mum for my pocket money, he turned and told me that nothing came so easy in his day. From the way he looked across at me, you'd swear he'd have preferred me to go out and get the loan of a horse than to get ten pence from Mum's purse to buy gobstoppers.

Anyway, a large farm stood next to Grandad Reilly's few acres. It was called Hunter's Farm and, even as young as fifteen, he had his eye on buying that 140 acres one day. The story goes that Grandad Reilly was farming his bit of land, growing turnips, tying corn and harvesting and working the flax until the Second World War came and the whole thing changed and with it the opportunity that he'd been waiting for arrived. 'They don't call people from South Armagh "wee and wise", for nothing,' he used to say.

One winter's evening, when the two of us were sitting watching a log in the grate that wasn't lighting because of the damp, he leaned across to slug a battered can of diesel over the bark. He sat back to watch the flames catch on and I looked over and I saw something soft flickering in him between the shadows and he began talking as if I wasn't there. Out of the bulk of him, the words came like sparks from wood that had to leap out from under the heat. Being a good judge of an animal, he must have sized me up rightly and seen how desperate I was to know a thing or two. He went on to tell me that years ago, when he was a young man, he would gather the milk from the cows, strain and cool it into creamery cans, then carry it up to the end of the lane, where a horse and cart would come and take it down to Ardvalley, 'in all sorts of weather'. He turned to me and I saw for myself the barnacle that was holding tight to something in him as he said, 'Carrying a twelve-gallon creamery can on my back, with milk spilling out and down my neck, by God, I can tell you it was hard-earned money.' Something in the old oak exploded and he unsettled the lot with a swipe of the tongs and said: 'When I got to the top of that lane and I saw Sammy Hunter's creamery cans on the back of that cart, knowing full well that McCulough the driver had driven up Hunter's gravelled lane and hoisted those cans on to the cart himself, well, I set my cap on owning that hundred and forty acres one day.' The log was crackling for mercy now and I rubbed my legs against the heat and looked across at him. From the side, his two eyes were like soft pools of oil and water mixed; you couldn't be sure if he was going to cry or explode into flames as he spoke. 'I can tell you now . . .' he said, '. . . there was never a milk-stained neck in *that* house.'

The next time I stayed over at Granny Reilly's, I waited up to ask him more about it. He looked at me and made a funny noise with his tongue and teeth like he had a bad taste in his mouth. He thought and sighed for a bit, then went on to tell me that during the war years, there was a law in the South of Ireland, under the new Free State government, that cattle and all animals, if they were bought and exported from there to England, had a twenty per cent duty on them. 'So what happened was the people, anyone who had their wits about them, bought the stock in the South and smuggled them up to the North, across the fields, up rivers, across mountains and wherever the path took them to avoid the Customs. There was good money to be made at that in those years.' The way Grandad sighed again and started rummaging around in his pockets for his rosary beads, I knew not to ask any more about it. Along with the crucifix, a sweet, wrapped in golden paper, popped out on to his lap. He tore it open and couldn't get it into his mouth fast enough. It was as if he had to sweeten the bad taste away before he noticed it.

One autumn, during the potato-picking season, Ger and I went to earn a few quid with the local schoolkids from round Granny Reilly's way. Our fingers were black and frozen and our backs were broken after only a week of it. I thought that was hard-earned money, I can tell you. One evening as we sat in front of the stove, I heard Grandad Reilly cursing beneath his breath: 'It was a hell of a time' and 'Jesus' and 'Ahhhh', as he bent to undo his leather bootlaces with the coal-fire tongs on account of the arthritis that crippled his bones. For a moment, I saw him there, a young man wandering against the current, up to his chest in river water, driving his cattle on, to sell in the North for a profit, and I figured I didn't know the meaning of hard work.

Barnacle Reilly. Sure enough, when he stuck to something, it didn't slip out from under him. The man who did himself proud at thirty-three years of age had enough land to leave to his five sons and enough money to educate his six daughters, leaving them to find their own way in the world.

Dad used to joke with Mum that the Reilly sisters might not have inherited land, but that they had inherited enough good looks and legs to reel in the richest men in Ireland. Mum would laugh and say, 'I'm still waiting.' One St Patrick's Day, when Mum and Auntie Breda were drinking hot toddies in our kitchen, I heard Mum say, 'No wonder we got lost, wandering around England with only a Catholic education in our pockets and enough men chasing us to fill an army.' They started laughing themselves silly, falling off the kitchen chairs like two kids. Auntie Breda was giggling so hard, she could hardly get the words out: 'It's one thing getting through life and it's another thing knowing something about it.' I didn't see what was so funny because Mum's sisters might have had looks and legs but from what I could see, they had as much luck reeling in a man as I had.

Firstly there was Auntie Katie, Mum's older sister by about ten years. Mum always said that Katie half-reared her. Anyway, she was one of the district nurses in her area, which was about three miles in every direction around Dunvalley town. She had emigrated to Australia a long time ago, where she'd married a man from the outback, but she came back to Ireland five years ago without him. I heard Mum say once, when she thought I was asleep on the couch: 'What good's a man who prefers shearing sheep to making love to a woman?' I didn't know exactly what she meant but it sounded like painful and dirty work to me.

Then there was Auntie Nora, the youngest. Dad said that Auntie Nora was so good-looking, half the country were chasing her if only she'd bother to look. Mum didn't like him going on about it but even I could see what he meant. But Auntie Nora never married and was always doing daft things like losing her purse or driving into lamp-posts. She was a member of the 'Cash and Carry' on account of her being in charge of the stationery store at the school where she taught. She went about once a month and bought things for her house like boxes of Fairy Liquid and mountains of tea bags. Walking into her hallway was like walking down the Cash and Carry aisle during the season's sale: cardboard boxes of everything from dried milk to plastic tumblers piled as high as the walls. Once they had this huge row and Mum told Nora that she'd be far better off if she found herself a man and started a family rather than throwing her money away on boxes of tinned soup that she ended up giving away to charity after their sell-by date. Auntie Nora told Mum to mind her own business. Mum kept shouting about her being 'a compulsive buyer' but if you ask me, they were all missing the point. What's the harm in buying a few extra cans of soup if you're always late for school and smelling of whiskey. Mum looked so relieved whenever Ger and I offered to keep Nora company on one of her shopping trips. I guess she thought we could look after her and she wasn't far wrong.

Dad said that all the Reilly sisters were as mad as bats. That would start a row like there was no tomorrow. Mum would go on about 'his mother this' and 'the crazy Devlins that' and right back to some Great-Great-Uncle Tom Devlin who used to wash his mouth out with soap to clean away his sins or something like that. It all got a bit murky for me to follow but it did get me thinking about things.

I know that a son or daughter can be like their parents. Our next-door neighbour, Micky Murphy, was so like his father that if he wasn't half his height, you'd think it was the same person.

One Sunday, his grandparents came in from Loughlow and I saw that Micky's father was the spit of his own father, which made Micky and his grandfather practically the same person. The only difference was that one stood straight and the other was doubled over with age. Anyway, that got me to thinking about where does the likeness stop. I mean, I couldn't help wondering about Grandad Reilly and his father and then his grandfather before him and so on and then I wondered, what if we were just all the same person living life over and over again inside different bodies, and it did my head in so badly that I decided to stick to the one idea – that I was like my Grandad Reilly; full stop. Hearing Mum and Dad listing off the nutters on each side of the family, he seemed to be the best bet of the lot.

It's true that whenever I saw an opportunity to make a quid, I wouldn't waste it. Take last autumn, when I needed new football boots: easy. Ger and I went out to Granny Reilly's orchard, cleared the apple trees and sold the apples around the houses in the neighbourhood for two pence a bucket. We made a profit and Mum gave me the rest to buy boots and Ger put her money towards a new football. Then there was the time we decided to set up a market stall outside the front gate, selling old toys, annuals and football cards. We were making money at it until, after an hour or so, old Mrs Byrne came out, shouting that she'd already phoned the Council to complain, so we had to pack up in a hurry. Our curtains parted and I saw Mum laughing at us from the window. She got a helluva kick out of that sort of thing. It was like I did things just to give her the pleasure of calling me 'Barnacle Reilly'. Now there's a thought to do my head in right and proper. I couldn't help wondering what it was like for Ger. I mean, she was doing the very same thing as I was, only you could see that Mum didn't get such a kick out of it, her being a girl and all.

One Saturday afternoon, Mum arranged to go to Belfast with Auntie Katie for a 'Homes Exhibition'. Ger and I, not about to waste an opportunity, planned to hold an *It's a Knockout* competition in the garden on the day that Mum was away.

During the previous week, we handed out leaflets to all the kids in the neighbourhood and the word got around like wildfire. We agreed to charge five pence entrance fee and make all the games and competitions free, except the orange juice and biscuits, which would be an extra one pence each. It was no problem wangling a trip to the Cash and Carry with Auntie Nora. We needed two large boxes of Fizzy Lizzy chews for prizes and it was always easy to throw on a box or two of what you wanted when she wasn't looking.

Pushing the trolley down the long aisles for Auntie Nora was the nearest thing to Hollywood I'd ever seen. She knew all the shelf-stackers and checkout boys; she looked like Elizabeth Taylor as she wandered from aisle to aisle like a movie star. She was in great form when we loaded up the car and even tipped the trolley-boy for helping us. Mum said it was just like Auntie Nora to spend a year in New York and come back with an embarrassing accent and a silly habit of tipping instead of a husband and savings. Anyway as we headed up the Dublin road, I was sitting in the back seat, between the boxes of soap powder, tucking into a Fizzy Lizzy. Suddenly Auntie Nora pulled the car over and disappeared inside McGuigan's, a pub, just outside Dunvalley town, about three miles from home. She parked up on the kerb, along the stretch of road where anyone who hasn't got money for the bus, stood to hitch a lift out of town. 'I won't be a jiffy, I'm just going in to see a man about a dog.' I looked at Ger, who looked at me; we knew the story too well. Dog indeed. The car was loaded down with spiral notebooks and enough soap powder to cleanse every sinner in the country. It turned out I was allergic to the stuff and in a matter of minutes I was sneezing and snorting like a sick cat. Great.

It was mental. I never realised until then how many people had to hitch a lift home. I noticed Mrs O'Sullivan from our estate, standing down from the bus stop, smoking like a chimney with one hand and trying to stop the traffic with the other. Her face was all screwed up but it was hard to tell if she was cursing every car that passed her by, or if she was just enjoying a smoke. The way she dragged so hard, taking it down to the stub in just under one minute flat, you could almost hear it fizzle. She worked at the hospital and if they didn't let her smoke inside, she sure made up for it when she got out. She caught my eye as she ran for a blue van, coat-tails flying, showing her service uniform underneath, and I know she was embarrassed. I didn't mind one bit about where she worked, it was the way her white hair was all yellow from the smoke that got me. Feeling sorry for grown-ups is just too awful for words.

Just then, three hard lads, probably from Carn Hill estate about a half a mile up the Dublin road, ran up to our car thinking it was their lucky day. Whatever they saw when they peered through the window, they didn't even ask for a lift or anything, they just looked at us funny and walked away, laughing, thumbs out and heads jerking round like cocky gits. I wasn't surprised; I must have looked a sight, all red nose and streaming eyes, and Ger was no better; she had a face on her like she was sitting on a bed of nails. Ger hated waiting for anything; even waiting to open the wrapping on a present made her mad, so I could imagine how she wanted to tear Auntie Nora to shreds. Anyway, we had no choice and about two hours later, she staggered across the road, arms laden with crisps and orange juice. She flung them wildly at us, then threw herself into the driver's seat. Ger looked across at me as the car jolted and stalled, then rolled down the pavement into the middle of the road. The bus honked at us from behind and when I looked back, the driver was waving his fist and cursing like crazy. Auntie Nora started giggling and Ger quickly grabbed the keys from the ignition and told her she was in no fit state to drive.

Just then, one of the hitchers ran over.

'You're Joe Devlin's lad.' I was sure he was looking at Ger.

'Yeah,' she answered.

'I'm Seany Caragher from the Moley road. I work in Kennedy's.' He pointed down the hill towards the pub, a different pub, where we'd often waited outside, in the car, on the kerb, until Dad had seen a man about a dog too.

'Oh yeah,' said Ger.

'Do you need a hand?' He took one look at Auntie Nora and you could tell he knew what he was dealing with. He looked like a man who had a lot of experience with that sort of thing and I felt relieved.

'Look, I'll drive you home, if that's OK with you and I can walk down to the Moley road from there.'

'OK, but you have to promise not to tell my dad about it?'

Ger knew she was taking a risk here, but it was one worth taking. He ruffled her hair. 'You're a good lad. I won't say if you won't say.' He smiled at us in a way that said: 'I know just where you're coming from.' It's the best smile that any grown-up can ever give, I swear.

Seany Caragher helped Auntie Nora into the back seat. When he touched her, she went all silly and floppy in a girlie way that was too daft to be just the drink, and you couldn't help but wonder when she'd been this close to a man before. Then, just as she lowered herself into the seat, she yanked her elbow away from his hand, quick as a flick-knife, and you could tell that whenever it was, it could hardly have been fun. When he took off, she rolled around between the sugar bags and the washing powder for a bit, then she sat herself up, leaning her head against the window looking up at the sky like a seasick sailor. When she started to sneeze I didn't feel sorry for her, not one single bit. We arrived home and Mum was out, so we got Auntie Nora in, made her hot tea and put her to bed.

I could have thought a lot about why Mum was happy to leave us with a woman hardly fit to tie her own shoelaces, but

I didn't want to. I guess, having a sister as lonely as that, must be as unlucky as someone pouring a packet of itchy powder right down the middle of your back; all prickly and no way to reach it. I knew what it was like to have an itch I couldn't scratch and I could only guess what it was like to spend a lifetime with one. I suppose, eventually, it just feels like home.

On the day of 'It's a Knockout', Mum set off early to pick up Auntie Katie and as soon as she was out the front door, we got to work. We spent all morning fixing up the garden, setting up the stalls, hanging up signs, cutting up sponges, boiling eggs, bending clothes-hangers, sorting out the timetable, making juice and collecting as many footballs as possible.

Footballs or no footballs, by two o'clock, we were as ready as we'd ever be. People were queuing outside the gate where Ger was sitting with a cashbox, ready to take the entrance fee. I gave her the nod and honest to God, the money started to roll in. I was too busy counting heads – eleven in the first batch – to notice that Spud, one of the first in, had headed straight for the jelly stand and was tucking in. I rushed over and told him that he had to wait for the jelly competition to start before he could eat.

'But I've paid my money, and you said everything inside was free. Look, it's on the poster.' His dad had something to do with the civil rights marches and would probably have been able to close us down on this small detail, so I offered him a job instead of an argument. I could tell from the numbers that we were going to need an extra pair of hands. I looked across and clocked the panic on Ger's face when Head-the-Ball Murphy and two of his cronies from the houses down by the bottom road had attached themselves to the end of the queue, jerking and twisting like a Chinese Fortune Fish on a sweaty-hot palm.

'Flippin' heck,' I mumbled. 'Look, Spud, if you help me, you can eat as much jelly as you like and I'll pay you five pence as well.'

He looked thrilled to be asked, like I was doing him a favour, and he agreed immediately.

'Wow. Sure.'

'Just stick by me and do whatever I say. First game up is Tug-of-war. Let's just get everyone into two lines, OK.'

'But on the timetable it says the jelly competition is first.'

'Sure,' I nodded, 'this is called thinking on your feet.'

'OK. Yeah, thinking on my feet.' As I rushed over to the Tug-of-war corner, he was at my heels like a puppy. He was so eager, I wished I'd just left him eating jelly. What the hell.

Doing the Tug-of-war was my way of gaining control before we lost it. Strange logic but it was better than no logic at all, especially when Head-the-Ball Murphy, better known to his mates as Spider, was at the gate, dancing on the balls of his feet, cocking his head from side to side, looking for trouble like he had a right to it. I could tell he was hassling Ger about the entrance fee. I was about to go over when I saw her wave them in. She looked back at me and shrugged. I agreed. What choice did we have? If we let them look around they might just leave.

I nodded, Spud blew the whistle and both teams hauled and pulled like fishermen reeling in a whale. I was watching Spider closely. We all knew he was a bully. He'd pushed around every lad in the neighbourhood and he had a trip-switch into nuttiness that was so quick, blink and you'd miss it, as he head-butted you to the ground. Watching him there, pulling at the end of the rope with all his might, his neck bulging with the strain, made me feel all sad inside. Daft, I am and I'm the first to admit it. He cracked a smile and it made him look like the rest of us, instead of a wee hard-man from the bottom road. You couldn't help but wonder why he chose to wear a face like all the life had been frozen out of it when you could glimpse something else, underneath, so close to the skin. Dimples? Good God. You can't be a hard-man and have dimples. No way.

Suddenly Team B tumbled back against the fence, one on top of another in a pile of bodies. Team A jumped about shouting and cheering like they'd won the pools. Amazing. It was weird the way Spider's face lit up when I handed him a Fizzy Lizzy; you'd swear he'd never won a prize in his life.

'OK, everyone, stay in your teams. It's Kick-the-Ball-through-the-Ring and may the best team win.'

'No, it's Eat the Jelly. Come on, fatso. Take the stand.' Spud looked behind him hopefully, then turned to face Spider and pointed to his chest as if to say, 'Are you talking to me?'

Spider had trip-switched and the air was freezing around him so fast, the icicles were already forming in my throat.

'OK, good idea. Eat the Jelly next, five contestants please,' I said but everyone ignored me as they shuffled around uneasily. One of Spider's cronies stepped forward.

'I'll eat the jelly. No fears,' he smirked.

I was beginning to feel like I was in the car with Auntie Nora at the driver's seat after all. We were definitely headed down the wrong side of the road and I could see a collision coming not far round the bend, when Ger, who'd been watching from the fence, started toe-tapping the ball. There she was, grabbing the keys from the ignition again and I have to say, I was glad it was her rather than me. The sound of her trainers against leather was so loud, all heads turned to see and Spud rose to the challenge.

'What a good idea, Keepie-Uppie. Let's have the Keepie-Uppie competition.' I figured he must have been good at it the way he was so keen.

Spider started and he did well to get to thirty-five. Ger was next, on the boy's team of course, and she made it to forty-five. I saw from his face that he was not a good loser.

'Best out of three,' I chipped in to try to save the day. I tried to catch Ger's eye but she wasn't looking at me.

Deliberately.

God Almighty, she wasn't going to push this one just to prove a point about girls being better than boys? Not now, Ger, of all times, not now, but the 'now' that most people would say 'not now' to, was the very 'now' that Ger couldn't resist.

Desie was about to start when Spider pushed him aside, grabbed the ball, walked up to Ger and poked her in the chest. There was some confusion on his face about what he was going to say next. I mean, he wasn't going to admit that he'd just been beaten by a girl, if indeed she was a girl and what did any of us really know anyhow?

'I've got one of those fancy boys here, lads.' He was strutting around Ger like a peacock and his cronies started laughing. I thought he looked funny too, but not that funny.

'Shouldn't you be over there with the little girlies then?' They all laughed.

'I'm not a "girlie", for your information.'

'Oh, so what are you then?' He didn't want an answer. He looked around at everyone and announced with a sneer, 'Doesn't know if it's a boy or a girl.'

Ger stood her ground.

'Boo,' he jutted his head forward into her face and she jumped backwards. 'Looks like it doesn't know if it's a man or a mouse, either.' They laughed again but Ger decided to give as good as she got.

'I'm as much of a man as you are.'

She knew what he was like. What was she doing? Was the sausage in her pants not good enough for her? Did she have to prove to herself that she was as much of a man as the rest of us by getting beaten to a pulp by Head-the-Ball Murphy? Jesus help us.

'Oh, the little man says he's as much a man as I am. Do you hear that? Well, we'll just have to see, now won't we?'

'We'll just have to see,' she answered back.

'Right. You and me, down by the garages, now.'

'Right.'

Down by the garages only meant one thing. Whatever Ger was hoping to gain from this fight, I prayed that the sausage was firmly embedded in its place because Head-the-Ball was the last person in the world we needed to find out about the Cookstown sizzling in her pants. That was one thing that neither of us would ever live down.

Everyone piled out of the garden and over the fence to get good standing room for the fight. They couldn't get to their ringside places fast enough; they weren't complaining or asking for their money back, that's for sure. The lads were all huddled round Ger, patting her on the back, getting her ready for the encounter of a lifetime, when out of the crowd, Wee Turkey Plunkett came hopping towards Ger as sparky as Jiminy Cricket. He was called 'Wee' because his dad was called 'Big' Turkey Plunkett. He was a butcher and while one look at the dad would put the fear of God into a living soul, Wee Turkey was so tiny and scrawny that when the two of them were walking together, you had to think of Laurel and Hardy and laugh yourself stupid. Anyway, Big Turkey was a real Muhammad Ali fan. Everyone, even Spider, knew that you didn't mess with the son of a man who taught his boy boxing moves in the front garden, with a butcher's knife sticking out of his back pocket, for all the world to see. He was all, 'Son, you gonna eat him up *and* his daddy too', and 'Don't forget it, son; get down *low* and *low*' as he moved around Wee Turkey, giving it all, two left jabs and a rapid cross around his face and shoulders.

One day, a few of us watched as he danced like a butterfly and stung like a bee around a dazed Wee Turkey, who was standing, jabbing at thin air with his leading hand. Big Turkey was sounding off like Muhammad Ali: 'He's trying to jab me, but I'm young, I'm handsome, I'm fast and I can't possibly be beaten' and 'People do say I'm cocky. People say I need a good whupping. Some say I talk too much, but I'm the greatest.' Anyhow, now Wee Turkey came hopping through the crowd, arms around Ger, like Ali's coach, 'Ger, remember, youse pretty, and he's ugly' as she made her way down to the garages, lost in a sea of bodies that hovered like bees around honey.

Spider had chosen the spot; he was standing solid in the far corner, close to the fence, with his cronies around him, all so hard you'd think they'd been nailed to the ground. Ger emerged from a swarm of arms and hands and was stood facing him. A circle formed around the both of them. Spider was twice her size. It was like she was featherweight and he was middle but you could feel that everyone was rooting for Ger and it almost balanced the scales in her favour. I was thinking, optimism is a good thing when faced with certain death and suddenly it all jump-started into life.

Our dad had a soldering gun for fixing radios and stuff. Well, Wee Turkey was as mental as mercury, coiling and melting into hot balls of rolling metal under heat, as he yelled orders at Ger from the side: 'Keep your guard up and your chin down' and 'Go on, jab, jab, jab with your left and in with the right cross' and 'Look at his eye, keep looking and *move*, Ger, *move* your feet.' Ger was dancing. Impressive. She was actually bouncing on her toes, shifting around Spider with her two fists up and jabbing. 'Go on, Ger, hammer him with a left jab; a rapid right cross and a left hook and he's mince.' I wanted to tell Turkey to put a sock in it but he was so strung out, it would have been impossible to reel him in. Like lightning, Ger was in like Flynn, punching with both hands at Spider's chest and chin. He came through swiftly and hammered her hard with a right hand on the side of the head. She pulled back and Turkey was yelling, all purple-faced, 'A good right hand, Ger, come back and hit him with a right.' Just then, Two-Lugs, old Mr Largey's Collie dog, squeezed himself through the crowd, barking, licking and jumping at Ger's crotch as excited as a kid on Christmas morning. She tried to shake him off but he had discovered Aladdin's cave in my sister's trousers and he wasn't taking no for an answer.

Spider saw his chance and as he moved in with both hands, he stepped on Two-Lugs' hind legs with his studded Doc Martens. That was his downfall. Every good fighter had a weakness and here he was, Head-the-Ball Murphy, about to fall from a nothing punch. I could almost hear the commentator above the roar of the crowd: 'Two-Lugs, the Gallant Challenger, is throwing everything he can as he dives at Spider's crotch.' The dog gave a whole new meaning to 'get down low and low'. Spider didn't know what bit him as he fell to the floor, but it has to be said, he went out like a champion, punching with both hands, landing a sting to Ger's head that had her on her back like there was no tomorrow. Spider was rolling on the ground, holding his crotch, wrestling with Two-Lugs and screaming for help. Everyone rushed around Ger; tears were sprouting from everywhere as the blood burst from above her left eye. Wee Turkey, Joe, Og, Desie and I lifted her to her feet, 'every inch a champion, you're every inch a champion'. Didn't he know when to shut it. Obviously not.

The crowd dispersed and trickled back into our garden. 'Let the games commence.' We'd studied the gladiators from ancient Rome and if they enjoyed a blood bath followed by entertainment, I decided to give it a shot. And it worked.

We sat Ger on a chair outside the back door and I ran in for hot water and towels to stop the blood. She was fighting back the tears but there was no need. We'd all been there and we knew. Wee Turkey legged it over the fence and up the road to his house. He was back within minutes with a lump of raw meat that was so fresh, it looked like it had just been cut out of the side of a cow. It probably had. He slapped it on to Ger's eye.

'This will do the trick', and who were we to argue? The steak fell over the side of her face and down around her ears; she could have passed for a cling-on from another planet.

'You're gonna have a bruiser,' I said proudly.

'So's he, plus he won't be able to pee for a week.' Ger, who was shaking all over, tried to laugh. 'Ouch.'

'Don't laugh.'

She smiled up at me and said in a cowboy accent, 'Like you say, Seany, a man's gotta do what a man's gotta do.'

I swear to God, it would have been too painful not to say it; but I didn't; I couldn't. But I thought it. I did. I thought it really loud, as I lifted the meat to check the wound: 'You're a barnacle, Ger Devlin. A real barnacle if there ever was one,' and I meant it.

Sometimes thinking things loudly is a better option than saying them.

Chapter Nine

After four weeks of sunshine and football, the Rice brothers arrived from Belfast. Their arrival had the effect of barley on hungry chickens. I'd often helped Granny Reilly to feed the chickens in the yard; one minute it was all quiet and the next, it was a flurry of beaks, feathers and feet, as the feed was scattered. Well, the Rices were the farmers and we were the chickens. The word got out that they had arrived and everybody who was anybody gathered outside their grandparents' house, clucking from pillar to post, waiting for them to come out and throw their handfuls to the wind. They were the only people I knew who could stop a football match mid-play.

Soon news got to us that Marty and Bernie had locked themselves into one of the garages behind the houses. From what Ollie O'Sullivan told us, they were inside, in the dark, lighting candles. It was worth checking out and sure enough, as soon as we arrived at the garages, Marty opened out the wooden doors, stood there and with fingers as long as sticks, he picked out a few of us by hand. I thought of Jesus Christ and his disciples and how they all just dropped their boats and nets and followed him. Marty Rice might not have been walking by the Sea of Galilee but I marvelled at how he had the power of Jesus to gather a group around him, as I wandered into the darkness with the chosen few.

They had dozens of church candles and a box of matches between them and soon we were sitting around in a circle, making hand moulds from hot wax and pulling ghost faces over the flames. Marty told us that he was coming to live with his grandparents and would be going to school in Dunvalley town in September. He'd been involved in an 'incident' a few weeks ago, when one of his mates, Liam O'Riordan, an older lad of seventeen, managed to get his hands on a rifle from a local drinking club on the Falls Road. One night, he and Marty were drinking snakebites outside the youth club when he told Marty that he had a Kalashnikov hidden behind the fireplace in his bedroom. Marty said he didn't believe him, so he went home to get it. They were pretty drunk and soon they were messing about with the rifle, playing Commandos through the estate, ducking and diving behind cars, pretending to shoot each other.

'Was it loaded?' asked Ger.

'Might have been for all I know.'

During the winter, Commandos was one of my favourite games, crawling through the gardens in the dark, rolling through hedges, firing our fingers for pistols at the enemy; but using a real rifle was the wildest thing I'd ever heard.

'Anyway, we thought no one would see us, I mean everyone was asleep, it was two in the morning but we were spotted by one of the neighbours who thought we were two UDA snipers. He called a few other neighbours and we were told later that we were nearly shot, until Liam's Da recognised us, as we were falling about under the light of a street lamp.'

'Jesus.'

'So, my parents had to go to this emergency meeting of the local council or something and they were told to get me out of town for a year or so, or they'd have to knock some sense into me.'

'Jesus.'

'What happened to the other lad?'

'Because he was seventeen, he was told to leave the country. He's gone to America to stay with relatives and he's not coming back.'

We sat in silence, teasing our palms through the hot flames and pouring molten wax on to the cement floor, with shadows flickering around us, licking their way up to the corrugated roof above our heads.

'Let's go,' someone said. 'It's getting hot in here.'

Football fell by the wayside for a couple of days. Last year, the Rices brought games from Belfast that we'd never heard of: Rope-Tig; Land-Sea-and-Air; Squeeze 'til You Drop and Spin-the-Bottle. Things were different when Marty and Bernie were around. For a start, more girls wanted to play than usual and this added a new flavour to the games. Twenty boys chasing

Dana O'Leary with a rope around the estate was much more fun than a few lads playing Touch-Tig up on the Green. Last summer, after they went back to Belfast in late August, we attempted to play the games they'd left behind but numbers fell off, the girls disappeared and the games went on hold.

I saw the way everyone looked at them: the same way they looked up at that statue of Jesus in the glass case, all other-worldly like they were from another planet. No fear; Marty and Bernie slotted into their rightful places of honour as comfortably as old pennies into a one-armed bandit.

After two days of Rope-Tig, it was time for Saturday's Big Match.

About thirty of us were messing about on the Green when Adrian moved to the goalposts to pick the teams. From out of the crowd, Marty emerged holding the ball. I looked across at Frankie and a wash passed over his face like a bad colour and I knew something had happened during the two days of tig, that no one was aware of at the time. There were no objections as Marty Rice was elected by popular vote and no ballot box to the position of Liverpool captain and for the first time, I understood that there could be much more to a game of tig than a game of tig. I had to admit that he looked the part and he had a way with him that made you want to give it to him. I envied this quality from a distance, like I envied those kids who lived in England and got on to *Jim'll Fix It* or *Swap Shop*. It wasn't a green envy, more like a sad one, that didn't really understand why I was never going to get my turn in the spotlight. Right then, I made it my business to keep a close eye on Marty Rice; I figured there was a lot I could learn from him and the first thing I noticed was how he chose my sister Ger as his centre forward every time.

The O'Rawe sisters were a mystery to us. They moved in a few years ago and didn't mix with anyone. They went to St John's, a massive comprehensive in Loughlow, and even the way they walked together in their pink uniforms to get the bus in the mornings, with their big ties and platform shoes, separated them from the rest of us. You could tell they had each other from the way they wanted nothing to do with any of us and that in itself was enough to make them an item of fascination.

Whether it was the heat or the arrival of the Rice brothers that set the sisters off, it's difficult to say. But, one baking afternoon, a week or two after the fight, Ger and I went up to the Green for a game and the place was deserted. The sun was melting the tarmac and young Sloaney Price from across the way was picking bubble gum off the road and eating it.

'What are you looking at?' He was touchy.

'You'll get worms doing that,' Ger shouted across to him.

'What happened to your eye? Looks like the dog's dinner.'

'Never you mind. Those stones will lie in your stomach for ever and give you cancer.'

'I'd rather die from cancer than go to Hell for touching Karen O'Rawe's slit.'

'*What?*'

'Frankie says that all the lads are going to Hell for touching Karen O'Rawe's slit.'

Frankie was his big brother.

'And where is Frankie?'

'He's down there, going to Hell with the rest of them.'

Sloaney was pointing towards the garages and we headed off to see what he was on about.

We turned the corner down to the bottom garages and sure enough, about fifteen lads were hovering about on the roof of the corner garage, next to the O'Rawes' house; shirts off, waving them above their heads and hopping around on the corrugated iron roof like they were doing a rain dance. It was so hot, they'd rather their feet melted than their football studs.

As we got close to the O'Rawes', we saw another dozen or so lads in the garden. One was halfway up the drainpipe; three were climbing the side gate that separated the front and the back garden; a couple were rapping the letter-box and then I spotted Frankie and about five others, peeking through the net curtains into the living room. The house looked just like the old lady who lived in a shoe, who had so many children she didn't know what to do.

'What's going on?' I shouted up to Desie who was hopping about on the roof.

'They've got the Rice brothers in there now.'

Jimmy, Adrian's older brother, had just come out.

'Jimmy says they're going the full way,' Og wasted no time filling us in.

'Who?'

'The sisters, they're going the full way.'

'Jesus.'

'And I'm next,' shouted Liam, Desie's older brother, 'it's me and Desie. We're next.'

'What you on about?'

'Look, they can see us from the bedroom there and they're picking us off like flies. Come on, get up on the roof so they can see you. Come on!' shouted Desie.

Suddenly the rainmakers on the roof started roaring and waving their shirts in the air.

'Look, look, there they are.'

I looked up and the net curtains in one of the bedrooms gently parted, like a crack that was forming under the weight of bodies hanging around the house. Then a hand appeared and the window opened.

'Move away from the door. Move away from the door or no one gets inside.' It was a girl's voice. A hand without face or body attached was speaking to us from a great height and as it disappeared behind the white veil again, the boys in the garden scrambled out over the fence to form a queue at the gate.

The front door opened and the two Rice brothers slipped out like two hind legs from a tadpole. One spring, I filled a jam-jar with frogspawn and made a pond in a plastic bucket by the back door: little rocks, river weeds and stones. I watched them for hours, lying there, thick as tapioca. I thought they'd died, until one morning I saw tiny fishtails darting about, then days later, legs, sliding out from deep inside the skin. Amazing and disgusting, all at the same time. I felt the same way now.

'What happened?'

'Did you get to see everything?'

Everyone was jumping frantically around them like pop-up toys but they just walked straight out the gate and across to Ger and myself, standing at the garage doors.

Liam and Desie were already dropping down from the rooftop. Desie was pulling on his T-shirt but Marty turned to him and said, 'Not you.'

'But we're next. They said.'

'Well, they've changed their minds.'

'That's not on, no way,' Liam protested.

Marty looked straight at Ger.

'They want you. You and him.'

He turned to me and I nearly died right there on the spot.

'What for?' I asked.

But they didn't answer. As they headed over the back fence of their grandad's garden, they looked like two cowboys striding out through the swing doors of a saloon after winning a shoot-out. I looked across at the red door. Number 11, Cherryview Estate. A door like any other door. But the sun, pelting off the red gloss, made it look like the fire of Hell was licking at the threshold. Terror bolted through me. I knew that if I entered there, I'd be heading into the Wild West too.

'But that's not fair. Desie was upset.'

'Look, you can go instead of me,' Ger said.

But there was no way out of this one.

'You must be joking,' said Liam. 'My dad always says, you have to give a woman what she wants or you're wasting your time.' Funny how dads are a mountain of useful information that's no good to you when you most need it. Resigned, Desie was back on the fence, scaling the side of the garage wall, reaching for the metal roof and hauling up his skinny bones again.

Ger looked as petrified as I did. She knew this was a serious case of 'A man's gotta do what a man's gotta do'. Either she came clean about the sausage in her pants or braved the challenge like a man. I asked myself what would Clint and the Duke have done, if faced with a surprise attack like this: they'd have tightened their gun-belts and faced the showdown. That's just what I decided to do.

'You first,' I gulped.

'Wagon's Ho!' I said it out loud, I did, and Ger looked across at me like I was crazy, speaking all American and that, but as I climbed off my horse and lifted my poncho, I could see her eyes glisten beneath her Stetson. They didn't call her 'Steely Eye Devlin' for nothin', I thought.

The Martini advert with the lovely lady, the hot-air balloon and that song: 'Any Time, Any Place, Anywhere' was the nearest I'd ever come to knowing about the facts of life. And I knew that there would be a time, a place, and a where, when they would all be revealed to me but I didn't think it would be in the bedroom of the O'Rawe sisters and me, speaking like Clint Eastwood with a six-gun in my pocket, when I was supposed to be playing centre forward against Man United in a Cup Final match up on the Green. It was all too much, too soon, somehow.

As we eased open the door, I strutted into the darkness. My spurs clinked as a voice called from upstairs, 'Lock the door from the inside.' I looked across at Steely Eye. She locked it. I could smell chips. Chicken and chips. Nice. I was sure Clint enjoyed a good chow-down after a shoot-out as much as the next man.

'Shooting, drinking and killing – that's my game,' I said to myself as I strutted upstairs and through the bedroom door. 'But pardner, this is a turn aside from the trail.' I'm sure I said it out loud because Ger stared at me again with an expression on her face that looked as bewildered as a lone ranger facing down the James Gang. Then she saw them too: sisters; both sitting pretty on the edge of one of the beds facing the door. Their long dark hair was down and they were all brown eyes and lips. They were so similar they could have been twins. One of them was looking at us and the other one wasn't. That was about the only difference I could see.

'What's your name?' asked the older one.

'Seany.'

'Not you.'

'Ger.'

'What happened to your eye?'

'A fight.'

'Sore?'

'You know.'

'Ger, do you want us to show you how to kiss a girl?'

'My brother does.'

Outlaws no doubt. We were old-time lawmen and now, for the first time since that tempting gold shipment, something was coming between us: women. The ruin of every good cowboy.

The shy one, Eileen, looked up and smiled.

'We can show you both,' she said.

Yeah, I thought, too trigger-happy for me.

'Sure. We'd like to know, wouldn't we, Ger?' I was still speaking in an American accent and I couldn't stop myself.

'OK then,' the older one, Karen, smiled at us. 'I'll be the boy, and my sister here, she can be the girl.'

Then she got up and squeezed past me to stand by the door, shoulder against the wall with her hands in the pockets of her flares like she was a cowboy chewing baccy against a cactus.

'OK, then,' the younger one said, as she patted the bed, 'this is a bench and I'm just sitting here, looking around and he wants to kiss me. What does he do?'

I was too busy worrying about an ambush to be able to answer.

Ger was speechless too. The younger sister giggled. 'Here, we'll show you.' Then she nodded to the other sister, 'the boy', who was waiting by the door.

'OK, ready?' she asked 'him'.

'He' nodded.

The 'boy', took a pace forward. You could almost hear the crickets; smell the dust.

'Oh! Hello. Is anyone sitting here?' 'He' gestured to the 'bench'.

'No, it's free,' answered the other sister.

'He' rustled along the mattress and sat down next to her, looking up at the clouds.

'Lovely day, isn't it?'

'Yes, it's a lovely day.'

113

'Did anyone ever tell you, you've got lovely eyes?'

'Well, you're the first.'

I wasn't sure which Western this was turning into or which way it was going to end but I remembered that the girl often runs out and gets shot in time to save the hero. 'Don't do it,' I yelled aloud.

The sisters jumped.

'You frightened the life out of me!' and 'Yeah, my God!' they said and they leapt with fright and grabbed hold of each other. All that hair so close together made them look like one girl with four eyes. Weird. A four-eyed girl and a Western was enough to make me feel mental enough to eat a bar of soap. For the first time I understood where that crazy Great-Great-Uncle Tom was coming from.

'OK, where were we? Oh yes,' they continued.

And one of the sisters started humming. It sounded like an Elvis song: 'I Just Want to Be Your Teddy Bear.'

As she came to the second verse, she slowly slipped her arm along the bedstead, behind her sister's back. I could hear the crickets now, loudly and clearly sending out their calls through the heat of the midday sun; the sound was deafening. Her hand appeared on the other side of her sister's shoulder and as her fingers gently landed on to her collar-bone, she pulled her sister to her. Like magic, the crickets stopped; Elvis stopped, yet the air was thick with sound. I held my breath as she bent her head down and like a bee landing on to a petal, she brushed the tip of her tongue across her sister's mouth and slowly parted the lips. It looked like she was eating an Oyster Shell ice cream, teasing the wafer open to get to the good bit. The younger sister sighed and slipped down against the pillows under the pressure. The older sister moved her head from side to side, then rolled over and on top. They were both moving a little now and sighing. It was the strangest thing I'd ever seen. They were kissing. Good God. The sisters were really kissing. And they weren't stopping.

The whole world fell silent around me; the only movement, their arms, their limbs, the heads and then the pressure. Good God, no; not the pressure. My mind was going blank and the sacred image of the Virgin Mary flashed before me. 'Hail Mary, full of grace, the Lord is with thee,' I was mumbling now but it was useless; it was too late to stop a thing. I was sure I would go to Hell for this; watching a boy, who was really a girl, kissing his sister. This Western was as wild as you could get.

It must have been a minute before they pulled back for breath. I could just make out a face from beneath all that hair. Jesus. I'd never been so shocked in my life; a gunshot straight to the upper thigh as I reached for my holster, then another to the gut as I stumbled backwards into the dust.

Not that they cared. They both sat up and rolled their lips together. As if to seal them down. But they were so full now that they just sprang back into shape. They were all hot and ruffled. I'd never seen anyone look like a ripe tomato before; you know, the kind that would burst if you as much as lifted it. Seeds. All those seeds that popped out when you held it in your palm. The younger sister ran her hand over her T-shirt, as if to straighten it out, and she sat up and smiled at me.

'Do you want to have a go?'

Do I want to have a go? I was trembling in the dust; confused and overawed, I could only wonder what would Clint Eastwood or John Wayne have done now? They'd have been so darned cool they'd have known just what to say: 'I gotta go catch me a gunslinger; another time maybe.' That sort of thing.

For a moment, no one knew what to do. It looked like they were about to start all over again. I could hear the lads on the garage roof. Someone was dragging football boots along the corrugated-iron folds. It sounded like a riot was starting. The younger sister turned to me again.

'Now it's your turn.' She patted the bed for me to sit.

'Would you like to be the boy or the girl?' she asked.

I was so uncomfortable I could hardly sit, never mind think, so I just said, 'You decide.'

I'd never sat so close to a girl before, not like this. The smell of her, she was sweet, I'll never forget it, as sweet as all the fruit gums in a box at once and she was asking me to take my pick.

Just then there was a racket from one of the other rooms. It sounded like a body clambering through a window. There was a loud crashing sound; something – a glass or a cup – had fallen and smashed against tiles.

'Shit.'

'Quick. Get out of here.' The sisters were in a panic. Ger and I ran out of the room on to the landing where we could see for ourselves: arms falling forward into the sink and legs dragging themselves through the tiny bathroom window behind. Desperate Desie had managed to climb the drainpipe and find his way in. Surprise, surprise.

'Look what you've done,' screamed the sister. She was talking about the smashed perfume bottle on the bathroom floor.

'My mum will kill us. What do you think you're doing?'

'It was my turn, that's all.'

'Get out, get out the lot of you.' The yelling from outside was getting louder and as the three of us were bundled out of the front door we knew that the game was over. Ger and I wandered through the crowd and just like Marty and Bernie, I didn't know how to answer the firing squad. 'What happened?' 'Did they go the full way?' 'Tell us, go on tell us.' But we just strutted our way outta there, and galloped off into the sunset.

Close to home Ger turned to me.

'What the Hell's wrong with you, speaking all American like that?'

'Is that all you can say?'

'There's not much else to say, you saw it same as I did.'

'Ger, have we just committed a mortal sin?'

'*Murder* is a mortal sin, Seany.'

'There's *mortal* and there's mortal, Ger.'

'What do you mean?'

'I don't know but I feel sort of strange, don't you?' I couldn't bring myself to say that watching *her*, kissing *her*, had aroused something in me that I'd never considered in my wildest imagination before. I was different, no doubt about it.

117

'It was pretty weird, if that's what you're asking.'

We were at the front door now and Ger reached into the letter-box for the key. She pulled it out on a long piece of string and slotted it into the keyhole.

'I guess that's one of the good things about being a boy; getting in line to kiss a girl like that.'

'I don't know.'

'Have you ever kissed anyone before?'

'No.'

The way she answered so fast, I could tell she'd been thinking about it.

'Ger, it looked kind of nice.'

'You looked scared stiff.'

'No way.'

'Yes way. You wouldn't have gone through with it.'

'Would you?'

'Sure.' Too fast again.

'What will you do if they ask us back?'

She didn't answer me.

Ger was right. I was as scared as I'd ever been. I knew nothing about girls or how to kiss them and I wasn't sure how much I wanted to learn now. All the same, I'd seen how that Eileen O'Rawe looked at me and I thought I should get some practice, in case there was a next time. I went into the bathroom, stood in front of the mirror, pressed my lips between my forefinger and thumb and moved them open and shut. It looked more like a silent war cry than a French kiss. I changed my mind, this whole girl thing would be better left alone until I knew what I was doing. There was only one place to go looking for information. I waited until Ger and Mum were out before going to see what I could learn from those glossy pages in the back of Dad's wardrobe. Something about getting close to the real thing had made those pictures too strange for words. For a start, there wasn't much about kissing in there; it was all straight in at the deep end and it freaked me more than ever. I decided, there and then, never to look in Dad's wardrobe again. When the promise of the real thing was as sweet and as lovely as the smell of fruit gums . . . who in their right mind would settle for less?

I went into the bedroom, lay on the bunk and the warm sun filtered through the open window on to my face. Hell or no Hell, I drifted off to sleep, dreaming of shootin', gamblin' and saloon girls . . .

119

Chapter Ten

As surely as the sisters had opened their door to the world, they shut it again. A few days later, I wandered down to the garages, and looked up at their house like a lovesick puppy. The curtains were drawn across the windows and it looked as if no one was home. Word got out that they'd taken the boat to England to see their grandmother. I wondered whether the sister, Eileen, the shy one, had thought of me; staring into the waves that pounded the ship, as it pulled away from the harbour. Mad. I am and I've said it before. All those songs about the Irish leaving their homeland for England and America were swimming around in my head and I fancied myself as Michael from 'The Fields of Athenry':

Low lie the fields of Athenry,
Where once we watched the small free birds fly,
Our love was on the wing,

We had dreams and songs to sing,
It's so lonely round the fields of Athenry.

My fingers were twitching as I tapped out the tune in mid-air.
Football was the only distraction for idle hands, and I ran up
the pitch to take up my position.

That Saturday before the game, Mum was busy stripping the
walls in the living room. Since Dad had gone to England, the
tightness about her mouth, like she was holding back a curse,
had softened and I noticed a light in her eyes that wasn't there
before. I ran into the kitchen for a gulp from the tap and heard
her humming to the radio in the living room. I went through,
water still dripping from my lip, and stood in the doorway,
watching her as she balanced herself on top of the chair, tearing
away at the wall like a crazy cat. She had piled the furniture
into the middle of the room, just like Scarlett in *Gone with the
Wind* when she had to leave Tara on account of the Civil War,
and a wild idea came into my head.

'Mum?'

'Oh my God, you frightened the life out of me.'

'Mum, couldn't we just leave now?'

'What are you talking about, son?'

'Pack up and leave before Dad comes back?'

She turned her back on me and continued picking at the
paper beneath the cornice. When she had it in her grasp, she
started pulling; it kept coming and peeling, like a strip of
sunburnt skin. She had to step off the chair and by the time it
reached the skirting-board, she was almost standing beside me

but she didn't look round when she said, 'If only it was that easy, son. Now wipe your mouth and go out and play. Don't let me see you 'til tea-time.'

I went out the back door, over the fence and up towards the Green where a kerfuffle was breaking out. The four large boulders, used for marking the goalposts, were missing and Smithy, a lanky lad from down by the houses on the main road, had accused Pod Maloney's dad of lifting them in the middle of the night for his rock garden. A circle was forming around the two boys, as Smithy insisted that he'd seen Pod's dad from his bedroom window, placing the boulders between his garden gnomes in the back garden. Pod, more of a terrier when aroused than you'd expect, was already sparring at Smithy and sparking for a fight when Marty stepped in and broke them up.

'Wise up, lads, nothing's worth breaking up a good partnership.' Marty was right. On a good day, Pod and Smithy were the Toshack and Heighway of the team. Breaking them up would have been as mad as doing a scramble in the school playground with your prize football cards. Pod got the last word as he pulled away and screeched at us like a nutter whose head was about to explode, 'My dad buys all his rocks from Flannigan's suppliers and I'll knock the block off anyone who says otherwise.'

'OK, OK lads.' Rice was still in control. 'That's settled then?' He winked across at Smithy, just to let him know that even if he was right, he'd best just leave it alone. Smithy trailed off the pitch like a wilted flower and hovered about on the sidelines until he had pulled himself together.

'We'll just get us some more boulders. OK, Bernie and Frankie, you two, go down to the main road; Liam and Sloaney, you go that way; James and Malachy, you two look down by McNamara's shop and Ger, you come with me, we'll go across into Boyle's, there's plenty of rocks in those fields down by the well.' Everyone split off into their groups and some of the lads went along with them to help out. Before I had time to think, Marty and Ger were making their way up towards the top road opposite Boyle's gate. I had an uneasy feeling in my gut about the way no one was hooking up with them, so I decided to run after them and tag along behind. After all, I had made it my mission to watch Marty Rice in action. He might have thought he could pull the wool over my eyes but I'd seen the way he'd been looking at my sister ever since he'd arrived: all, 'Ger this' and 'Ger that' and whatever action he might have had up his sleeve down at Boyle's well, I was going to be there to witness it.

On the other side of the gate, the poppies whispered about in the barley and gently melted towards us like a trickle through a Raspberry Ripple. Then the wash of colour spread like a breaking wave, tempting us into another world; a world away from tarmac and concrete and into the smell of green. I wanted to run through the middle, leaving a trail behind me that ended in a circle of flattened stalks, from where I could lie back and look at the clouds, but Boyle was always on the lookout for intruders and he was the last person you'd choose to interrupt your dreams, with his dogs and pitchfork. I noticed Marty and Ger tripping ahead, one behind the other, like two cowboys kicking at stones and I couldn't help sensing that there was

123

something between them that didn't include me. I raced to catch up, when suddenly Ger sprinted ahead.

'Brilliant,' she shouted back to Marty.

'This one will do.' Marty ran towards Ger who was standing by the well, with her foot on a large boulder: the perfect goalpost. I stood back and watched as they got down on their hunkers and shoved, all breath and limbs, heaving the boulder out of its resting place. 'One, two, three, and . . .' the thing swaggered on to its side, revealing a circle of yellow grass, alive with scuttling creatures like a decaying doughnut around a great black hole.

'What's that?'

'A hole,' I said.

'I can see it's a hole but *what is it*?'

'One way to find out.' Marty leaned over and his arm disappeared into the ground up to his chin. He turned to Ger, 'I've got something', and he carefully hauled up a long, thin object, wrapped tightly in sackcloth and bale cord. Ger rushed to his side and together they untied the cord, folded back the cloth and held it between them like a freshly caught trout, gleaming in the afternoon sun.

'A sniper's rifle.'

'Jesus.'

'It's been here a long time, at least a year.'

'What do we do?'

'The IRA use them to pick off Brits. We put it back, that's what we do or they won't think twice about using it to pick us off.' Marty knew what he was talking about.

'Jesus.' Ger spat on the hem of her T-shirt and started rubbing frantically at the barrel of the gun but Marty snapped it back from her.

'Don't do that, for Chrissakes, you'll set the thing off.'

'Get our fingerprints off it.'

Marty looked at Ger straight and said, 'The IRA don't shoot girls.'

Ger's eyes flashed black.

'I'm not a girl. I'm a boy.'

'You look like a girl to me.' His eyes were on fire as he lifted his hand, gently brushed the hair back from her face and bent to kiss her on the lips. I'd never seen air so thick with something that I wanted to put my hands into and stop the flow. They looked like two goldfish from where I was standing; mouths all gaping and wet behind the gills. When he pulled back, Ger dropped her head down like a nun in prayer. She didn't fool me though. Watching Karen O'Rawe kissing her sister was one thing but watching my sister, who was really a boy, kissing Marty Rice was something else all together.

The sound of a tractor from the top road made us all panic.

'We have to get rid of it, quickly. Throw it into the well.' Ger was pulling the gun away from Marty and he was tugging it back. He fell backwards and the gun bolted straight up into the air like a prize goalpost.

'No fucking way. Ger, we have to put it back or we're dead meat, you understand.' The sound of the tractor was getting louder and as it trickled along the road towards Boyle's gate, Marty broke into a sweat. We held our breath and to our relief the tractor rolled past and on, up the road towards the Green.

Marty looked straight at Ger, 'We have to do this slowly. It has to look exactly as we found it.'

The folds in the cloth and the indents where the cord had hugged the rifle for months were so clearly marked, it was as easy as replacing the Sellotape around the top of a tin of Quality Street, after you'd taken out the green triangles. Marty and Ger got to work and within minutes, they were standing with an unopened rifle in their hands. Marty leaned down and placed the gun into its hollow, as gently as he might put an injured fox back into its lair to save its life. He got up and nodded to Ger and like all the best mid-field partnerships, without a word between them, they lifted the boulder and placed it on the spot, no dribbling, just one clean right-footer, off the boot and into the back of the net.

'Let's get out of here.'

We bolted along the track towards the gate and leapt over the bars as quickly as Speedy Gonzalez. Marty turned to Ger, 'We'll tell them there weren't any, OK?'

She nodded. In the distance, on the Green, Bernie and Adrian were carrying a boulder between them, that was big enough for two.

'We could smash it with a hammer,' Ger was still out of breath.

'Spud will stand in for one match,' I said.

They both turned and stared at me as if they'd seen me for the first time.

'Look, Seany, we don't breathe a word about this, *any of it*, to a living soul or you're dead, do you understand?' I knew what he meant.

'Marty, we could tell our dads; *something*.' Ger was flustered.

'Ger, I'm telling you, they'd tell us to do exactly what we've done. What can they do, remove it? No. They'll get shot for doing that. Tell the RUC? Ehh, no, they'll get shot for doing that. We've done the only thing we can do, understand?'

She turned to me. I could tell by her voice that she was trying to convince herself as much as me. 'OK, Seany, we have to forget this ever happened, we don't want to create any problems for Mum and Dad, OK?'

Ger glared at me long and hard. I wasn't sure whether she was talking about the gun or the kiss. I wasn't going to mention the gun to anyone but I knew I had some ammunition tucked into my back pocket, if Ger ever used Dad's magazines to blackmail me again. I swore to her that I wouldn't mention the gun to a soul but I saw that she still looked uneasy about something and I knew that the gun wasn't the only thing on her mind. I would have been all mixed up, too, if I'd changed from being a girl one week and then kissed a boy the next. That put Ger in the same league as the O'Rawe sisters, only worse. I was beginning to think that all this heat was getting to her and turning her head to marbles. And I was getting annoyed; she was messing with my head too. I mean, what the hell was going on I'd like to know. It looked like she couldn't make up her mind any more about what she wanted. I, for one, could see the tiny buds pushing through her T-shirt. Last summer, she'd taken her T-shirt off, but now, well, you couldn't help noticing that no matter how hot or sweaty she was, she kept it on.

All things considered, I decided that it might not be such a bad idea to be a girl after all. *Turn yourself back and get on with it, Ger.* The more I thought about it, the more irritated I became. Girls are made of sugar and spice and all things nice and what are little boys made of? *Please.* Girls are *soft.* Boys are rough. Girls are *beautiful.* Boys are spotty. Girls are *clever.* Boys are daft. Hell, why would anyone want to be a boy? My sister must have been mental, that was it, pure mental to want to be a boy. I was feeling more and more angry with her; the way she ate her boiled egg in the morning, tapping all around the shell before taking off the top, *how annoying*; the way she had to double-check all her studs were tight before tying-up her boots, like she was George Best or something; *just get on with it.* Oh, stupid Ger, why don't you just be a girl and get on with making yourself beautiful and sweet like the rest of them?

Chapter Eleven

That night, Mum was taking Granny Reilly to a dance in Bridgecross and Auntie Katie was 'baby-sitting'. After Mum headed off, Auntie Katie made herself a cup of cocoa and put her feet up with a box of Jaffa Cakes after 'a long hard day'. Every day was 'a long hard day' to her, otherwise I might have felt sorry for her. She offered me a biscuit and I headed out to the steps, to clean my boots. Ger was up to no good, writing letters to Elvis in her room. She was hoping against hope to persuade Auntie Katie to let her watch an Elvis film, which started at nine o'clock.

We knew all about Auntie Katie's work. Whenever she came over, she'd talk and talk till the cows came home about this patient and that one. I figured she talked so much due to coming from Sydney without a husband and all, but Mum said, man or no man, Auntie Katie could talk for Ireland. I didn't mind one bit, I loved her stories about crazy old ladies with bedsores, who'd once been nannies in America; or girls out by Loughlow Lake who got stones stuck in their fannies and had to have them removed with tweezers, and even people who got strokes. Don't get me wrong, I didn't like that they were in pain, not one single bit, but it made me wonder about their lives and what brought them to it. I once asked Auntie Katie all about strokes and she said that people got them from thickening blood that caused clots, that burst the walls of the arteries. She told me about a patient, a Mr Connell, who got one so bad that his whole body and face froze like a corpse. Now, I just got to thinking about all that clotting going on inside Mr Connell's body and started to wonder what might have been going on outside his body too. When I asked Auntie Katie about it, she looked startled.

'What do you mean?'

'I mean, was he clotting on the *outside* too?' She paused as if I'd given her something to think about and she patted my head.

'You are a strange little boy, Seany, but to tell the truth, Mr Connell was a mean old bone, not an ounce of mercy in him and I guess he had more clots in his soul than he ever had in his body but don't say I said so.'

'Why was he so mean?'

'God alone knows but he looked like a man who'd had all the love beaten out of him.'

'Like a car wreck?'

'Yeah,' she smiled, 'just like a car wreck.'

See what I mean. It's well worth asking questions for the answers you get.

Auntie Katie didn't usually look after us when it was her weekend on duty, just in case there was an emergency call-out, but it happened so rarely that she agreed to do it for Granny Reilly's sake. When she arrived, she told Mum that all her patients were done and dusted for the night and that there was nothing to worry about. But as luck would have it, just as she was finishing off the last Jaffa Cake, and settling for the night, the phone rang and she was called out to attend to an old lady, down Leightown way. It might have happened rarely, but here I was, stuck like a piggy in the middle between an Elvis movie and a crisis.

'Don't worry about us, we'll be just fine,' said Ger who was thinking of *Viva Las Vegas*.

'I can't leave you, your mother would murder me. Look, grab a sandwich, quickly now, and come with me.'

'Honestly, Auntie Katie . . .' Ger was doing all the work.

'"Honestly" nothing! Your mother told me you weren't to sit up watching that Elvis trash and I'm not about to leave you to it. Now hop to it. Besides I'd be arrested for leaving you two here on your own.'

We were in the car in minutes and driving along the back roads towards Leightown.

'Is somebody hurt, Auntie Katie?' I asked.

'Old Mrs Hughes has taken her bandages off and is wandering around the roads in her nightdress. She's a divil that

131

one, as mad as a coot. Some people don't know whether you're trying to help them or hinder them, I swear.'

'Has she always been like that?'

'Aggh, old age does funny things to people,' and with that she started flicking switches and changing gears and I knew not to ask any more. Old age. The lights of a car were coming round the bend towards us; darkness at first then the beams, striking the ditches and trees, searching for life, then '*Whoosh*' as two piercing eyes threw shadows into the front of the car and across our faces. I looked over at Auntie Katie. She looked old to me.

We hurtled along in silence. Ger was sulking in the back seat, pretending to be asleep. Everything about her was annoying me now. *Snap out of it, girl.*

Suddenly, we trundled up into a ditch, alongside a gate, and I noticed a small house through the bars. I blew against the window and traced the lines of the gate with my finger.

'Hop to it, you two, I can't leave you parked-up in the ditch like this. I want you to sit in the kitchen and not a peep from either of you, OK?'

As we were shutting the car doors, the neighbour ran up, apologising for calling Auntie Katie after-hours, but she didn't seem to mind.

'It's OK, Elizabeth, where is she now?'

'She's out the back. She's ranting, the bandages are off and her legs are in shreds, she wouldn't let me near her, Sister.' Elizabeth looked like she was about to cry and I thought Auntie Katie was going to have two patients on her hands but she

132

gently touched her on the shoulder. 'Now don't you worry, Elizabeth, you did the best you could, you were right to call me out,' and that seemed to calm her. She nodded and stared up at Auntie Katie with a round face and eyes so wide and full, she looked like a great big moon on legs.

Auntie Katie told us to go inside and wait. I pushed the door, and shoes and tin cans clattered in a heap on to the stone floor. She must have piled them high from the inside against something coming to get her. I covered my nose; the window in the kitchen opened out to the back of the house but the smell of celery and cats was so strong, even an open roof wouldn't have cured it. We could hear old Mrs Hughes before we could see her; her voice, coming from the back of the garden, was as brittle as a smashed-up eggshell but her words were strong: 'My husband's been fighting fascism all his life and I won't recognise the Crown now he's gone, you hear me, I won't do it.' We moved slowly towards the window and in the moonlight, silhouetted against a disused tractor by the outhouse, a frail bony figure, white hair sticking up and out, was punching and thrashing out at something, like a drowning body gasping for air. Then I saw – reams of bandages covered in muck and blood were wrapped around her fists and she was wrestling with them as if they were an enemy that she had by the throat. I'd never seen anything like it in my life.

Auntie Katie and Elizabeth came into view, tripping along the stony path by the side of the house, holding on to each other for support. And their eyes were on her too; she looked

133

as sinewy and as prickly as a blackthorn bush. Once, scrambling over a ditch in a hurry, I landed feet-first into one and I was picking the thorns out for over a week. I wasn't surprised they were approaching with caution.

'Come on now, Mary. Come on now,' said Auntie Katie gently.

'Get away from me, you're wicked, you hear me.' The two women were moving in on her, rounding her up from either side.

I'd seen Uncle Charlie tempting a stubborn calf through a gate in exactly the same way.

'No biting now, Mary, you hear me, that's a good girl. It's Sister Katie and its time to get those bandages on.'

Mary turned and stared at her, as startled as a starving child. I'd seen the faces on the Lent boxes for starving babies in Africa and I'm sorry to say but it's true, old Mrs Hughes suddenly looked as sad and as petrified as that.

'Get away from me. Get away.'

'Now, Mary. Come on now, there's a good girl.' Auntie Katie was talking as if she was a naughty child.

'Get away from me, I said.' Mrs Hughes was still punching air.

'I'm going to have to get cross with you, Mary. Come on now. Let me help you inside.' Auntie Katie was closing in on her gently. Ger and I leaned against the window frame and watched as she slowly reined her in; a bewildered creature, lost from the herd.

Auntie Katie was close now and she gently took old Mrs Hughes's two fists and lowered them to her side. She unravelled the mass of bandages from around her wrists. 'Now, let's get these off, OK, there's a good girl.' Mrs Hughes started to cry. 'My John, he's going to come back and he'll give you a piece of his mind, Sister, he went to the war but he'll come back one day and he'll tell you what's what.'

She was sobbing now and as she lifted her two hands to rustle her white hair into place, the old lady seemed to be raising her arms in surrender.

'Now, come on, Mary, John fought against Franco and he came home with all those medals, didn't he?'

'He did. He fought and he was proud of it.'

'And he had a good life, didn't he?'

'He did.'

'Well, let's sing him a little song, shall we? What's that one, the one you love?'

The old lady hesitated.

'Go on, Mary, sure you've a lovely voice, go on,' and Auntie Katie started singing to encourage her. 'Come on now, Mary, "Six long months I spent in Dublin, Six long months doing nothing at all."' Slowly Mrs Hughes joined in and they were both singing now, '"Six long months I spent in Dublin, Learning to dance for Lanigan's Ball . . ."' as Auntie Katie led her across the grass and into the kitchen through the back door.

When the door scraped along the flagstone, Ger and I bolted for the kitchen table.

Old Mrs Hughes stood in the open doorway and smiled as if she was expecting us. 'My hair, oh dear,' she feathered her fingers around her head again and I thought I saw a wren darting out and into the night behind her. It was the cobwebs by the gable there, and herself, would have made anyone see things that weren't there.

'Don't you worry about your hair, it's grand, Mary.'

'Lovely boys, are they yours?'

'No, I had to bring them with me, they're my sister's.'

'Lovely boys.'

Her skinny legs were all cut and bleeding and she could hardly lift them from the floor as she shuffled over to Ger and smiled.

'What a handsome boy,' and she raised her hand to my head, 'two handsome boys, she's blessed, your mother, she's blessed.'

'Come on now, Mary, let's get you into bed and we'll fix up those legs.'

'Not before I show these two boys my medals. Go on, Sister, pull that biscuit tin down for me, would you?' and she pointed up to a battered old box on the shelf above the fireplace, next to the egg stands and the salt.

'Here, hand it to me, Katie, hand it to me.' The old lady grabbed it from her and pushed it into my chest.

'Go on, open it, son, open it by the lid.'

I pulled the lid off and there, wrapped in old tissue paper and tin foil, like faded biscuits, lay a handful of medals. I didn't dare touch them in case they crumbled.

'Go on, touch them,' she said, 'take them out. My John, he fought fascism all his life. Look,' she pointed up to a framed picture of a man on the wall next to a photo of the Pope.

'Karl Marx,' she said.

'Come on now, Mary, let me bathe those legs.'

It was as if the picture of that man on the wall and the medals gave her something, because she turned to Auntie Katie, all shiny as a new pin, and said, 'You can do my bandages if I can watch Elvis.'

Auntie Katie smiled at Ger. 'There's one young man who won't object to that.'

They coaxed Mrs Hughes into the next room; two steps forwards and one step back, like the dance of the three old ladies. It was funny. Ger followed behind, darting here and there like a shadow that didn't know which way to go. When they finally made it across the threshold, she glanced back at me, threw her eyes up and left me alone with the medals. Laying them gently back between the folds of tissue, I swear I could hear sounds of gunfire, of men screaming and women sobbing. I'd never met Mr John Hughes, but sitting there at his kitchen table, I could feel his fingerprints wearing down the metal, rubbing skin and bones into the surface, as if to erase memories that were so sharp, they left him with little else to hold on to. I was beginning to feel old myself.

I stood in the doorway, looking through at Mrs Hughes sitting in her chair by the television, watching Elvis in *Viva Las Vegas*. Auntie Katie was bent over a bowl of water and Mrs Hughes held her legs out in front of her as if they didn't belong to her. She was belting out a number, looking as happy and as settled as any old lady you'd meet on the street. Only we knew better. Auntie Katie washed and dressed her wounded legs and when the job was done, it looked like the old lady had a layer of new skin all the way from her ankles up to her knees.

Ger was disappearing into the sunken sofa. I could just imagine her, years from now; as wrinkled as a dried gooseberry, huddled over, waiting for someone to bandage her wounds. The thought sent shivers right through me. She sat there, watching Elvis without a flicker of joy and I wasn't one bit surprised that she looked ill.

'You're tired, pet,' said Auntie Katie when she saw Ger's face.

But I was thinking, I'd look sick and tired too if, for a second, there was any chance of me ending up like that. I'd rather be an old man, dead in my grave, who'd fought fascism and had medals to show for it, than an old woman with nothing to do but wander around in the middle of the night, with only a biscuit tin, and a fight that wasn't even hers, to keep her on the straight and narrow.

On the way home in the car, I sat in the back with Ger.

'I'm sorry, Ger,' I said.

'What for?'

'I've been so annoyed with you, wanting to be a boy and not wanting to be a girl.'

'Yeah?'

'Well, after tonight, I don't blame you one bit. And there's something else: the very thought that Eileen O'Rawe might be ancient and batty one day, it's put me right off her, like *totally* off her.'

138

'I know what you mean.'

We bundled along the windy roads and fell against each other for comfort. Passing headlights flashed through like an opening between ditches and doors; then it was gone; like *gone* and everything was black until the next time; then *gone* and the pitch black descended again like a fairy-tale. And it came through; a discomfort like the pea in the princess's mattress, and I got to thinking about Auntie Katie and the way she had handled old Mrs Hughes and I leaned forward before I fell back again. 'It's been a long hard day, Auntie Katie,' I said. She smiled at me from the mirror and I knew I'd grasped the nettle before it had time to sting. '"The Princess and the Pea,"' I said.

'What?' Ger mumbled.

'I know what it's about: "The Princess and the Pea".'

'That's great,' and we rolled on home.

Chapter Twelve

Our house was like a snooker table; one minute all the balls would be perfectly still and the next they would be scattered in every direction, reds and colours cracking off the floor and walls, spraying patterns around the room like splattered paint. You never knew when the cue was going to strike but the one comfort I had was no matter when, or how hard it hit, until the balls stopped rolling, both Ger and I were going through the same stuff as we cowered together, watching from the cheap seats. Granny Reilly said she called us her 'Dunvalley twins' because there was only ten months between us but I think it was because we knew what the other was thinking half the time.

Sometimes, I'd look at Ger and she'd look back at me and I swear, I'd just get up and pour her a glass of Ribena or milk or whatever and she'd just say 'thanks', like I'd asked her what she wanted. Other people might have thought it spooky but

I didn't give it a second thought until that day, after finding the gun down at Boyle's well, when I knew that Marty Rice was stirring something inside Ger that had nothing to do with me.

Mum had finished decorating downstairs and the house looked like new. Before tea, we helped her to rearrange the furniture in the living room, which meant we ate our beans and toast watching *Doctor Who* from the sofa in Dad's corner and Mum sat admiring her matt finish from Dad's chair next to the door. Moving furniture was as exciting as going to Butlins for a week and coming back thinking your house was bigger and better than before you left. Mum let us stay up late to watch a cowboy film and for a moment, I imagined how happy we would be, the three of us together. My fantasy was short-lived because Dad came back two days early from England and staggered in the door just as the cavalry were coming to the rescue and Ger and I scarpered to bed.

'Do you think Elvis was a better kisser than the Duke, Ger?'

'Shut up.'

'Just askin', now you've got all that experience.'

'I'm warning you, you swore not to mention it.'

'Did not. I swore not to mention the gun.'

'What's wrong with you? Just shut it.'

'Ger loves Marty Rice, Ger loves Marty Rice.'

She wriggled down from her bunk and tackled me from the side. We tumbled on to the floor with a thump and Mum was up in seconds.

'Come on, you two, lights out. Have you said your prayers?'

She knelt down by the bed. 'In the name of the Father and of the Son and of the Holy Ghost, Go placidly amid the noise and haste and remember what peace there may be in silence . . .' This was Mum's favourite prayer and we joined in as best we could.

'Now lights out.'

'Mum, is it OK to say a prayer even if it's not a Catholic one?'

'Seany, sweetheart, a prayer is anything you want it to be, it's a conversation with God. Go on, you say a prayer, anything you'd like God to hear.'

I closed my eyes. 'Dear God, keep us all safe from harm. Amen.'

'That's lovely, now go to sleep.' Mum kissed us and left us in the dark. God must have been listening because we all slept soundly that night and, for a day or two, I really thought things had changed for the better but on the third day, the cock crowed and I cursed the Father, the Son and the Holy Ghost when the snooker balls started flying again.

I woke as soon as the key turned in the lock and Ger's feet landed on the floor, next to my head.

'Ger?'

'Shhhh. He might just go into the living room and sleep.' She tiptoed to the door where a slither of light from the stairwell lit up her eyes and I could see the fear. Then came the shout from Hell to waken the dead.

'Anne! Anne! Get down here now!'

'Jesus, Ger.'

I hardly had time to pull the blankets back, when I heard a thud on the staircase that sounded like the hound of the Baskervilles tearing its way up to the landing. Within seconds he was in Mum's room. A few moments passed, then her terrified screams went straight through me.

'My hair, Joe. My hair.'

'Get out of bed now.'

'Joe.'

'Get down on your knees, you whore.'

I ran to the door and both Ger and I clung to each other, shaking from head to toe like newborn piglets.

'What's he saying, Ger?'

'Not now, Seany.'

'Get your children in here now. *Now*.'

Mum's screams pierced through the wall and it sounded like he was skinning her alive as we tore back under the blankets.

'Not the children, Joe, not the children, please.'

'Your children have a right to know what a whore their mother is. Get them in here now.'

The bedroom door burst off its hinges, as it bashed against the bunk bed. I was curled into a ball with my hands over my ears, when the covers were whipped back and we were dragged out of our beds with Mum pulling and screaming at him, 'Leave the children alone, Joe, leave them alone.' Dad bundled us on to the landing as he fell backwards against the door frame.

He was so drunk, I didn't recognise his face. His eyes were drooping one second then out on stalks the next. He stumbled across the landing, falling from side to side between the wall and the banister, with the words slurring out over his lip, like spittle in a rattling old man. He looked like someone who'd taken leave of his senses. Everything about him was so far out there, I wondered whether he'd ever return to planet earth again.

'Get in here,' he shouted as he grabbed at Mum and fell on top of her on to the floor. We watched, frozen to the spot, as he dragged her across the room by the hair, shouting in her face, 'What did you say? Don't you ever tell me what to do with my children, you hear me, you whore? You hear me?'

'Yes, Joe, I hear you,' she screamed as he pushed her head away and staggered towards Ger and me, huddling together by the door. He grabbed us both by the shoulders as he ranted at Mum, who was scrambling to her feet.

'You don't deserve to be a mother. Tell your own children, go on, you don't deserve to be a mother.' Ger started to whimper and I was shaking so badly, I'm sure the tears didn't know which way was out.

'Get down on your knees.' The tears were pouring down Mum's face as she got on to her knees.

'Don't touch the children, please Joe, don't touch them,' she begged him.

'*Don't touch the children*,' he mocked her, 'that's sweet coming from a whore of a mother who would give away her only son as quick as look at him.'

'Joe, please don't . . . not now please.'

'Now, let me see you choose. Which of your two children are you going to give away now? Which one?' He held me out to one side and he held Ger out to the other like two scrawny chickens on show.

Mum was begging him on her hands and knees. 'Please, don't do this Joe, don't do it to us.'

'*Don't do it to us. Don't do it to us,*' he mocked her again. 'It's a bit late for that, isn't it? Now, choose. You get to give away one of your beautiful children, which one will it be? *Which one?*' he yelled as Mum lunged at him, pushing him backwards into the wardrobe. She gathered us to her and tucked us under her arms like a mother hen. I could tell she was gaining strength from us.

'Leave the children out of this, Joe, leave them out of it.'

He stood there snorting, 'You whore. Choose one of your children. *Choose.*'

Mum covered our ears and pushed our heads so tightly into her ribs, I could hear her heartbeat.

'I keep them. I'm keeping my children,' she screamed at him.

'What a pity you didn't say that fifteen years ago.'

'Shut up, Joe. Shut up, we buried that a long time ago.'

'You might have buried it but when I was in England, I tried to resurrect it. But you made sure I'd never be able to do that, didn't you? You didn't even put my name on the birth certificate, did you?'

Suddenly, the hurricane died as quickly as it had come to life and Dad stood there in front of us, head dangling down,

145

hands reaching for the wall. The debris was all around us: the broken wardrobe, handfuls of hair on the linoleum, Mum's torn nightdress, and I knew that it would need more than a miracle to repair the damage.

'Get out of here,' he nodded to the three of us. 'Get out,' and Mum scuttled past him with Ger and me attached to her side like a spare set of legs. She hurried us into our room and helped us into bed. I was shaking.

'Are you cold, son?'

'No, Mum.'

'I'm sorry.'

'Dad said you would give me away as quick as look at me.'

She started rubbing my hands, 'Ger, Seany, Dad didn't know what he was saying, he was acting like a crazy man. I'm so sorry.'

'But Mum, he said you would give me away as quick . . .'

She held me to her, 'My darling boy, he is saying things to hurt me and to hurt you and it's just not true, it's just not true, my Seany, you have to believe me.'

'Why does he want to hurt us, Mum?'

She held my head between her hands. 'Dad doesn't mean what he says, it's the drink talking, do you understand?'

I nodded, 'Yes.'

'It's over now, go back to sleep.' I laid my arms down along my sides and she tucked me in so tight I could hardly breathe.

God forgive me but if I had had Micky McKee's telephone number, I would have called him there and then and told him to come and finish off what he'd started. I lay there in the dark, feeling like a mummy in a tomb. Alive and not alive at the same time. I knew from our Egyptian project that they believed the Pharaohs never really died, even though they'd stopped breathing.

'I wish I was an ancient Egyptian,' I whispered to Ger.

'Why?'

'That way I would never have to worry about dying.'

'Go to sleep, Seany.' And I did.

The following morning, Mum was at the cooker, cracking shells into the pan. I watched her from the bottom of the stairs and the smell of bacon and eggs went through me like pins and needles. Everything looked the same but something was different, like when the summer ends and there's one cool day when it hits you that it's not coming back. I shivered. If ever she saw you shiver, Granny Reilly made the sign of the Cross and said, 'Someone's walking on your grave.' I never believed her until that morning, when I could feel those heavy footsteps on my bones and I knew that nothing would ever be the same again. The sound of water gurgled down the plughole and Mum said without looking at me, 'Your eggs are ready.' I really hate that. No matter what I have to say to people, I stare at them so hard they have to look away.

Later, Auntie Katie arrived and told us she was taking us to Granny Reilly's for a day or two. She sent us up to pack a few things, while she made Mum a cup of tea in the living room.

*

Last summer, when we went to Granny Reilly's for the long weekend, we chased the car all the way to the lower meadow at the bottom of the hill, waving as Mum and Dad disappeared into the distance, over 'Lunny's Hill'. Then we trampled our way through the brambles and stood there in the shade of the apple trees, grinning at the wide-open green space, before breaking into a run, arms out like airplanes, hopping and jumping until we fell exhausted on to the daisies. Every day, Uncle Charlie let me ride on the tractor down to Newtown to count the cattle. He said he wouldn't take Ger on account of her being a girl but she just ran behind us and jumped on to the axle, holding on for dear life, until he had to take her into the cabin too. In the evenings, I helped him to move the cattle from one field to another with sticks, but my favourite thing was collecting the eggs from the chickens in the battery. It was so loud in there, with the noise of the fans and the screech of the chickens, you couldn't think about anything except placing the eggs as carefully as possible into cartons, without cracking them.

But this time it was different. When we arrived, Granny was clearing up after the workmen had been in for lunch. There was turnip and ham left over, so we sat in the living room and finished it off. Auntie Katie closed over the door to the kitchen and I could hear her speaking to Granny in hushed tones. I looked across at Ger but she was too busy tearing at the fat to notice.

I tried to cheer her up.

'Are you going to tell Uncle Charlie you're a boy, Ger?'

'If he doesn't take me with him to Newtown, I'll just have to.'

She looked like she couldn't care less.

Auntie Katie soon left for work. After we threw our things into the back bedroom, we walked down the road to the lower meadow, crossed through the barbed-wire fence and into the open space. I ran ahead, arms out, shouting back to Ger, 'Come on, this is great', but she just stood there by the apple trees, staring into space like a lost sheep.

The following morning, the weight of silence hung about the farm, as thick as butter. The sounds of cows and pigeons melted their way through from a distance, more like a lullaby than a wake-up call. I curled down, nose cool from the freshness of mist and soil that mingled through the open bedroom window like a stony soup, wondering what had gone through my mother's mind, lying there as a girl, with the same smells of morning seeping up the sounds around her. Could she feel us tugging at her, way back then, as the quilt, soaked with scarlet fever, quarantined her from the rest of the world? Could she hear us whispering, through the long, wet blades outside: 'Come on, Mum; come on, Mum; come on through?' Granny Reilly always left the windows open. She said that fresh air was a cure for all that ailed you. I'm sure it had to do with how close my mum came to death, once.

And just like that, as I was snuggled there thinking about death, it was rolling its way along the country roads towards us;

a strange turn that would take our minds off the living for a while.

We got dressed between the blankets and shuffled down for breakfast. Granny was bent over double, peeling a mountain of potatoes into a bucket. She turned the handle of her knife towards Ger, wiped her hands on her apron and got up to skin the porridge. Outside O'Riordan's bread van skidded through the gravel, like hailstones whipping against a window with your face flattened hard against it. We ran out to sign for the order and carry in the fresh bread.

Before we reached the van, Mister O'Riordan, the baker, was out of the driver's seat in a fluster, rushing towards the house. 'Ger, Seany, is your grandmother in?' We followed him to the house and he told Granny that he had just delivered the bread to Old Rooney up the road and found him dead on the sofa; sitting up in front of the fire, with the pipe in his mouth and his dogs about his feet, as if he was still living.

'God, have mercy on his soul.' Granny Reilly blessed herself and we knew by the way she looked at us that we should do the same.

A wake sounds like a serious thing for most people, especially for the guest of honour, but my granny was always going to a wake here or there, in some part of the country or other. I never knew a woman who knew so many dead people.

Mister O'Riordan was a bit shaken and in need of something to knock him into his senses but Granny Reilly knew just what to do. She told him that she would send up Uncle Charlie to sit with the body but that he was to drive into town and tell Dr

Murray to come immediately. Then she poured O'Riordan a cup of tea and told me to run out to the van and bring in a packet of Snowballs from the trays. O'Riordan said not to worry, that he wouldn't charge her for them, and Granny Reilly fired a wink at me because she always said O'Riordan would charge you for the crumbs if he could. God forgive me but right then, I thanked Old Rooney for dying because there's nothing in this world like dipping a Snowball into a hot cup of tea, on a cold morning. After we'd sucked the coconut from between the tea leaves, Granny sent Ger up to waken Uncle Charlie and she started ringing around the neighbours to let them know.

Uncle Charlie took the Land-Rover up to Old Rooney's farm and soon after he was out of sight, Ger and I followed him up, to have a look for ourselves. Old Rooney lived in a small, whitewashed cottage at the end of a long dirt track, about a quarter of a mile from Granny's farm. He kept a few cattle, some sheep and chickens but I'd heard Granny say that he was half starved, half the time. Sometimes he'd call in on a winter's evening, for a drink or a meal, and Granny would rustle up something for him without Old Rooney saying a word. I knew nothing about him until that morning when Granny Reilly and O'Riordan talked about him over Snowballs and I learned that he had lived on his own since his wife died many years ago and his only son lived somewhere over the border, with two grandchildren who we'd never met.

Ger and I approached the cottage from the fields like two Commandos and leapt over the wall in front of the yard. Uncle Charlie's Land-Rover was parked in front of the window. We peeked inside. Old Rooney was sitting up on the sofa next to Uncle Charlie, who also had his eyes closed, and between them it was hard to tell which was the living and which was the dead. Then Uncle Charlie started talking to Old Rooney. I looked at Ger and she shrugged her shoulders, just as we heard a car coming down the lane. We darted behind the Land-Rover as Father Murphy, the parish priest, parked and entered Old Rooney's with a brown paper bag rustling under his arm.

We peeked again and saw him shaking Uncle Charlie's hand. He opened the brown paper bag and removed a large bottle of whiskey, took a swig and handed it to Uncle Charlie. Uncle Charlie said something, then reached for a cup on the dresser behind the body, filled it from the bottle and placed it firmly into Old Rooney's stiff hand. Being dead was the best excuse for a drink I'd ever seen. Uncle Charlie sat down again and said something to Father Murphy, bent his head low and blessed himself.

'Jesus, he's saying confession, Ger.'

'Don't be daft, you can't say confession with a dead body watching.'

'Well he is.'

Mortified, we scarpered over the wall and ran back towards Granny Reilly's house. From the field, we saw another car bobbing along Old Rooney's dirt track. The news was out and the neighbours were arriving to pay their respects.

That evening, Granny Reilly got dressed in her best and Uncle Charlie drove us all up to Old Rooney's. The small cottage was jammed with so many people, talking and drinking, you'd have thought it was a wedding, not a wake. Father Murphy had contacted Old Rooney's relatives in Dunford and his son, his daughter-in-law and their two grandchildren had arrived down with a truck-load of drink from across the border. From the number of bottles of vodka, I figured there'd be more than one dead body in the place by the time the night was out. When we went inside, Christie Cole was sitting by the door, in his wheelchair, with a glass in his hand, greeting everyone like he was the host. He nodded to Granny and Uncle Charlie and thumped Ger and me so hard on the back, we nearly joined Old Rooney in the next life.

'God bless youse, God bless youse. You're the spit of your mother, young Geraldine, the spit and God knows she's a fine-looking woman, never a better one stood in this county . . .' Ger was cornered but she didn't seem to mind, so I wandered through and on up the stairs, into the bedroom where the body was laid out on the bed, as straight as a board. A man, deep in prayer, was kneeling on the nearside of the bed, so I crossed over and knelt next to Old Rooney's head. I'd seen him many times over the years but I'd never seen him this close up before. Mrs Ward could have given an entire geography lesson on his face. Patterns meandered in criss-crosses along his forehead and down the sides of his cheeks like a dried-up river-bed. From the hairline, down through the centre of his forehead, a crevice as deep as a rift valley ran towards a dip in the bridge of his nose. He must have broken it once. Sad that. The way a man can lie there at the end of his life and someone as daft as me can sit there and think of parallel faults and rift valleys instead of praying for his departed soul. I shock myself sometimes, I really do. I heard footsteps on the stairs, which was just as well because I quickly headed back to the kitchen before I started looking for Lake Turkana or Mount Kilimanjaro.

Ger was talking to a boy of about fourteen and a younger boy of about nine. Old Rooney's grandchildren. The oldest boy was called Ernie and if you asked me, he looked like someone who didn't know when to rein himself in. Within seconds of meeting him, he gave me a wrist-burn and he thought it was funny too. His younger brother Michael seemed all right but he didn't say much, so it was hard to tell. I guess, because we were the only kids at the wake, we ended up sitting out in the backyard, chipping stones at the barn wall and talking about stuff, though it was hard going because Ernie kept interrupting and bragging, about things that you knew just couldn't be true and worse, things that you couldn't prove: like he told us he'd had sex with girls. Sure.

Anyway, he said he had this great idea and I wanted to hear it, I really did. 'Why don't we go in and nick a bottle of vodka and a bottle of orange from under the table and sit out in the barn telling ghost stories?' I thought it was the daftest idea I'd ever heard but I didn't have a better one, so I said nothing and Ger nodded, 'OK.' I don't think Ger would have agreed if Ernie hadn't referred to her as my 'brother'. She would have sold her soul to the Devil himself if he showed up and called her a boy. Anyway, Ernie had the whole thing so well planned, you'd swear he'd been organising it for weeks. As instructed, we all went inside and stood around the drinks table, while young Michael crawled underneath to stuff the bottles under his jumper. Standing there, shuffling around the table, my heart was racing and I got a rush about the whole thing.

Just then, Rosie Cassidy started edging towards us. Rosie Cassidy was as old as a rock but Granny Reilly always said, while she might be old, she was as sharp as a new blade. I couldn't tell if her eyes were lively from the whiskey, or from watching what we were up to, but when she looked across at us, I was like a rabbit caught in headlights.

'Ernie Rooney. Well, where's young Michael?' She was looking him straight between the eyes, as she grabbed my upper arm for support.

'He's upstairs with Grandad.'

'Oh, God bless youse. I'm sorry for your troubles. To lose such a good man.'

She was searching his face for something, as she shifted her weight from my arm to my hand. Her fingers, tight as a wrench, locked over mine and I almost toppled over when she pushed herself away and balanced herself back on to the stick.

'Thank you, Mrs Cassidy.'

'Ah Rosie, Rosie will do. I knew him well, a good man, indeed he was, a good man.' She was settling herself on to her two feet now, then she turned to me. 'Annie's boy . . .' she smiled, 'you're . . . a fine lad.' Just then, Ernie pulled out a handkerchief from his pocket, buried his face in it and started to cry. I felt a tug at my ankle as Michael, who was burrowing around on the floor, gave me the sign. I kicked Ernie as planned

155

and he turned to Rosie with eyes as wide as a young calf's and said, 'I think I'll just go outside for some fresh air. Ger and Seany, would you mind coming with me?' Rosie looked at us and said, 'Of course, of course.' She reached to touch him kindly on the shoulder but he had already turned away. That killed me. Whatever thrill I had, disappeared as quickly as the last breath from a dying pigeon. Telling lies was bad enough but telling lies to an old person was too bad for words. The whole thing went through me like pins and needles and for the first time ever, I knew what it felt like to need a drink to wash away my sins.

Before I knew it, we were sitting in the barn, on bales of hay, slugging vodka from one of Old Rooney's cups. The taste was so awful we choked it with orange cordial, which made the whole thing worse again but we drank it anyway. Some light was coming through the half-open barn door and the strange shadows that it threw across Ger's face reminded me of Old Rooney's corpse, so I was pretty spooked before we even started. Of course, Ernie was the first to show off his ghost stories and I had to hand it to him, it turned out he knew how to tell a good one. He started with this one about two Black and Tan soldiers who died in the very barn we were sitting in, where they'd seen something so horrific that they dropped dead of fright. His voice went loud, then quiet, then loud again as he made the strange sounds of the 'thing' that turned and ate them alive, leaving no trace of their mutilated bodies. Something was moving along my upper thigh and I jumped off the bale and fell on to the floor in terror. Even Ger rolled about laughing and I guess it was one way to pretend she wasn't as petrified as I was. Ernie was better than the rest of us at ghost stories, so we let him continue and soon I was so freaked out, I was knocking back the vodka to numb the fear.

When I fell backwards on to the floor for the second time, it was more than fright that kept me there. The beams in the ceiling were spinning around like a windmill and I turned away and puked up all over the bales of hay. Then I did something really stupid. I started blubbering like a baby. Ger was trying to get me to stand up but I was crying so hard, I just crumpled on to the hay, like a colt that couldn't find its legs. From where I lay, I saw Ernie and Michael stepping over the puke, backing out of the barn, staring at me like I was a weirdo. I couldn't stop thinking about Old Rooney, lying up there, with all those furrows in his brow and his own grandsons telling ghost stories in the barn outside, like nothing had changed. It made me shiver all over.

'Everything's changed, Ger, everything's changed.'

'Come on, Seany, let's get you out of here.'

Old Rooney's mongrel was sniffing around my ankles and it would only be a matter of time before someone else came to check out the racket. Ger threw my arm over her shoulder, dragged me out into the yard and bundled me over the gate into the field. My body landed with a thud on to the grass; I fell back and looked up at the full moon hanging there, throwing silver light everywhere, making the night sparkle like Heaven. I'm pathetic, I swear, but I almost started blubbering again, just thinking about Old Rooney who'd never see the moon again.

'Do you think Old Rooney is looking down on us?'

'I don't know, Seany.'

'Everything's changed, Ger.'

'Seany, he's dead. It's natural to die.'

'But everything's changed, Ger.'

'It's OK, Seany.'

'But Ger, things will never be the same again.'

'I know, Seany, let's get you home.'

I was thinking about Mum and the eggs breaking into the pan but I couldn't say.

We stumbled through the weeds to the house. In Granny Reilly's warm pantry, the embers were fading in the grate. I rustled them with the poker but there was no life there worth saving, so I placed the dry log in my hands back on to the hearth.

'No point wasting it,' I said to Ger.

'No point wasting it, Seany.' She helped me on to my feet and up the creaking stairs to bed. As I made my way in the darkness there, I couldn't get Old Rooney's face out of my mind: that steep-sided rift valley; a crack in the earth's surface, formed millions of years ago when the crust was being pulled apart.

A few days later, Auntie Katie came to pick us up. It was baking hot as we drove towards the house and the smell of freshly cut grass rushed through the open windows. As we passed Mrs Fern's house, the Rices and about a dozen other lads were in the garden, weeding and cutting the long grass with clippers, getting it ready for mowing. We pulled around Tinley's Corner, down past the Rices and on round to our house. I saw Ger's face before I saw the house.

'Why are the curtains drawn?' she asked.

'Your mother's resting, Ger, OK.'

'Why, what's wrong?'

'Nothing's wrong, she just needs a rest. I'll be looking after you for a few days, that's all.'

That's never all.

The house was pitch-black when we went inside and Auntie Katie whipped back the curtains in the living room to let the light in. I winced from the shock of sunlight and looked around for signs of life. The dust particles flitted about in the light and it looked liked nobody lived here at all.

'Where's Mum?'

'I told you she's resting.'

'Where is she?'

'She's upstairs, in bed. Now run along outside and play, she won't be awake for a couple of hours yet.'

Auntie Katie looked at her watch like she knew at exactly what time Mum was due to wake up at. Strange.

'But Mum never rests in the day.'

'I know, love, but she is resting today and I want you two outside until tea-time, so I can get some rest before my night shift.'

Auntie Katie wore her nurse's voice like she wore her uniform, and I could tell from her manner that she had put it on as soon as she'd entered the house.

Outside, in the heat, while we were pulling the dandelions from Mrs Fern's flower-beds, I turned to Ger and said,

'Mum's ill, isn't she?'

'I don't know.'

'Auntie Katie's got her uniform on.'

'I know but you know what Mum always says about her.'

'I know – "once a nurse, always a nurse" – but this is different.'

Later that evening, after tea, Auntie Katie told us that we had to wait until tomorrow to see Mum. She left us strict instructions not to disturb her while she went out to check on a diabetic she was worried about, out by Loughlow way. We knew not to ask about Dad; whenever Auntie Katie was around, Dad wasn't. That's just the way it was. He was probably at his mate's house in Dunvalley town and he wouldn't be showing his face while Auntie Katie clucked about the place like a mother hen. She told us she'd be back within the hour but that she wanted us in bed before she left. I heard her rummaging about in the medicine cabinet before she went in to Mum's room. A minute later, she was outside our door. She tapped it gently, 'OK, you two. Good night. Sleep tight. Don't let the bugs bite.'

When she banged the front door after her, I thought the walls would fall in around me. I'd seen it once on television, and it had made me laugh at the time.

'Ger, what's the name of that Charlie Chaplin film where . . .'

'I don't know.'

'That's all you've said since we got home, "I don't know." You must know something.'

I knew not to say much else. Ger's silence was as loud as a curse and I lay there as tense as she was. I thought of the Romans lying in catacombs underneath the Vatican. One Easter, Granny Reilly went on a parish trip and sent us a postcard of the tombs, lined one beside the other, like Victoria biscuits in a tin. I was in my box, Ger was in hers and Mum was way over there in hers. I was a 'jammy dodger', Ger was a 'chocolate bourbon' and Mum was an 'orange sandwich' in gold wrapping. I didn't want to open the wrapping and I didn't want to leave it alone. God help me, but I think of the strangest things when I want to. I decided to lie there all night dreaming of biscuits, when Ger shuffled out of her box and switched the light on.

'Ger, I can't sleep with the light on, OK?'

'I'm thinking.'

'You don't have to think with the light on.'

'If you want to know, I'm asking Jesus, Elvis and Neil what they think.'

'Well, surely the Holy Trinity can think in the dark.'

I whipped back the covers and flicked it off again.

Then the rustle, as Ger leaned across from the bunk to the wall and flicked it on.

I leapt out and flicked it off. This time, I stood there waiting. When her hand came across, I grabbed it just before she reached the switch.

'Look, smart alec, the light stays on.' She punched my hand away and stabbed it on again.

I quickly snatched her wrist hard and twisted it. I did. And I

161

mumbled beneath my breath, 'Some boy you are; afraid of the dark.'

She thrust her other hand forward and seized a fistful of my hair from above. 'What did you say?'

'I said, some boy you are, OK?'

I tried to pull her hand away but she wasn't letting go.

'Take that back. Take it back.' But I wouldn't.

I grabbed her arm with both hands. Within seconds, she had tumbled out of the bunk on top of me and we were scratching and kicking on the floor. We rolled across to the fireplace, a ball of limbs and knees, like cartoon tumbleweed down a lonesome road. By the time we hit the hearth, Ger had wriggled herself on to my chest but I was holding her head between my hands, nails and fingers squeezed tightly over her cheeks.

'Look who's talking,' she screamed at me through the pain. She was thrashing her head from side to side, trying to shake me off. Her cheeks were turning red, then white in tiny patches between my fingers.

'What's that supposed to mean?'

'I want a proper brother, not a wimp like you.'

'*What's that supposed to mean?*' I yelled at her again.

She managed to slip her knees on to my upper arms and from there, she squeezed my elbows down into the sheepskin rug on the floor. I jerked my hips up and threw her into the air like a rodeo rider. It was useless; she was holding tight to the saddle and in a mood to tell me what was on her mind.

'I want a proper brother. OK? Not some girlie who follows me around like a sheep.'

There was only one reply to that.

'And I want a proper brother. Not some half-baked girl who thinks she's a boy.'

She dug her knees deeper into my arms. The pain was shooting its way through my elbow joints and up to my throat as I struggled to get away.

'And some boy you are when even your own mother wants to give you away.'

There it was. The sting. And I fell for it.

'What do you mean? *What do you mean? What do you mean?*'

As I repeated the question over and over again, I wrenched my right arm from her grip and stabbed the heel of my palm under her chin to try to stop her; but the words just kept coming.

'You heard Dad; Mum wanted to give you away. I hope she does it sooner rather than later.'

'Shut up. *Shut up. Shut up.*'

I tried to push her head back but she twisted herself free.

'I'd rather have no brother than a brother even Mum wants to give away.'

Ger's eyes were bulging and her face was twisted like crazy Giant Haystacks on Saturday-afternoon wrestling. I used the only ammunition I had left.

'Some brother you are, kissing Marty Rice down by the well, you'll go to Hell for that.' I must have hit her weak spot; when her grip slackened, I threw her off like a prize bronco.

And I did it. I punched her in the stomach.

163

Just then the door swung open.

Mum rushed to us and pulled us apart.

'Stop it, you two. Stop it.'

Ger was in tears, holding her tummy on the floor, but something came over me. I was spitting fire like a volcano I'd seen erupting on telly and I had to get the last word.

'I want a proper brother, Mum. Not her. She's not even a boy.'

'I am. Mum, you tell him. I am a boy.'

'You are not.'

'Am so.'

'Are not.'

I could feel my face swelling up beneath the skin and my eyes were all hot in their sockets as I fought to stop the tears. For a second, everything calmed down, then Ger panted through the stillness,

'Mum, I want a proper brother, not one you want to give away.'

And that was it. I lunged at her again, only this time Mum rushed in to stop me and I ran into her nightdress, hitting out at her with my fists.

'Dad said you wanted to give me away. I heard. He said you wanted to give me away.' Mum pulled my face towards hers and she frantically rubbed my cheeks together between two closed fists, as if to wash away a stain. Then she closed her eyes, threw her head back, took a deep breath and looked across at Ger. A strange thing passed between them. I'd heard that silence before and I remembered:

'*Seven for a secret never to be told.*' And Mum whispered:

'You have another brother, Ger.'

Then she looked at me.

'You both do.'

I could hear that magpie flapping its black wings and I cupped my hands across my ears to stop the sound.

What are you talking about?

What are you talking about?

I was screaming inside.

Mum slumped on to the bed and collapsed over as she held her face in her hands.

'There. I've said it.'

She was speaking to someone who wasn't there.

Who was she speaking to?

She raised her head from between her hands and stretched her mouth across her face. She was all teeth and slanting eyes. It was the same face she'd pulled when she'd stood in the Butlins Hall of Mirrors. This time, no one was laughing.

'There, I've said it. *I've said it!*' she shouted now and turned to face the Sacred Heart of Jesus with eyes so full of something, I couldn't bear to look.

She was speaking to Jesus.

'I've said it. And the world hasn't ended.'

She shouted up to him again: '*And the world hasn't ended!*'

I have to say that she looked as if it had.

A darkness crumpled around her like a heavy cloak and she peered at us with tiny eyes from beneath the hood, as her back hunched over under the weight of it. She let out a heavy sigh, then hung her head down between her knees.

'Mum?' I said.

Mum didn't move her head; but her fingers were twitching, reaching out towards us and she uttered a word.

'Son.'

At first, I wasn't sure, then she said it again.

'Son.'

I wanted to go to her but Ger held me back with her arm and she moved to take Mum's outstretched hand. As soon as their fingers touched, Mum let out a groaning sob that sent pins and needles right through me.

'Ger, my darling son.' Mum was mumbling through the tears and I didn't like it one bit.

'Gerald, my beautiful boy. My darling beautiful boy.'

Gerald? I thought, *who is that?*

'My beautiful boy, I'm so sorry, my baby boy.'

Ger was kneeling by the bed now and it crossed my mind that her wild story about Herod and the Unionists might just be true after all.

She touched Ger's cheek, 'Two years older than you, my darling girl.' Then the sobbing started again as her head fell forward.

'What do you mean, Mum?' Ger asked gently.

Mum looked at us both from that falling place; and then I heard it. A gentle, distant splash as the pebble hit the water. There they were: the ripples, rising and falling in waves on the surface, out from the centre, to the whites of her eyes that were ruffling at the edges.

Then everything went still, like she was telling us a bedtime story, and she spoke all soft and full of whispers.

'He was beautiful. So perfect. Just like you, Seany, with a head of black wavy curls and eyes . . . Ger . . . I was young, too young . . . I held him in my arms, my boy, my Gerald, then I let them take him away. Do you understand?' Her eyes were reaching out, desperate, searching for something.

The ripples; the ripples; that was all I could see; the ripples, still flowing out from the black. And she continued.

'It was my first year at nursing college . . . Liverpool', she smiled, '. . . every young girl's dream', and she touched Ger's face in a funny way. 'I was nineteen . . . the nuns, they told me he was going to a good family, a professional family and I let them take him . . . I was frightened . . . I didn't want to marry your father . . . I was so frightened . . . and . . . God help us . . . my father would have murdered me . . . murdered me . . . and then your father . . . he was too fond of the drink even then . . . and . . .'. She turned her head away.

She started sucking her lips together, as if she'd just taken a bite from a bitter lemon. I thought the words would choke her.

'Jesus, what could I have done, what could I have done at the time? Then we were married two years later . . . will you ever forgive me . . . born on your father's birthday . . . he will never forgive me . . . your father will never forgive me.'

She dropped her head again between her hands. Her sobs went through me like daggers and my heart was freezing over with the sound of them.

'And they took you away . . . I held you for five minutes and I let them take you away . . . Gerald Reilly,

167

your name, that's the only thing I left you with. A name . . . I'm so sorry, my darling boy, I'm so sorry.'

I wanted to run over, drag Ger away and shut the door behind us but I couldn't move; feet nailed to the floor. Again.

Mum lifted her head. 'There isn't a day goes by when I don't think about him, wonder where he is. I tried to find him but . . . I don't know . . . they didn't keep the records back then . . . I have to live with it . . . please God, I hope he's safe and happy and . . . you two . . . my treasures. Seany, do you see? *Do you see, my love?*'

I nodded, 'Yes, Mum' and the tears just started all over again.

It was as if she'd waited all this time to let them out and there was no stopping her now. My ears were on fire. I felt as if I was going to throw up but I just stood there, a jammy dodger, well and truly out of its biscuit tin, not knowing what to do with myself. There was no mistaking the words she was saying, 'My boy, my beautiful boy . . .' as she cupped her two arms across her body, holding a newborn baby to her breast.

'All mixed up and numb.' Granny Reilly used those words once, to describe a spring lamb whose mother had died giving birth. We took her in and bottle-fed her until she was strong enough to go back to the flock. I wanted to do the same thing for Mum.

Minutes later, when she had stopped crying, I saw; and the falling place was gone.

For a moment I could hear the gentle sound of laughter filtering through. I guessed it was how she'd been, before all this had happened. I'd never seen her look so young. She smiled at us, pulled Ger gently towards her with one arm and reached across to me with the other. I folded into her.

'I love you both. I love all my children.'

She held us so tightly, for a moment I was scared she would never let us go.

Everything about jigsaw puzzles makes me depressed. You don't know you've lost a piece until you've almost finished and then there's this gaping hole in a beautiful boat scene, crying out to be filled. One day, when you find the missing piece beneath the sofa, you don't want to put it into the picture and spoil something you've just grown used to. A boat with a gash in its hull becomes interesting, when you think about it. I'd rather walk in the rain and come home soaking wet than do a hundred-piece jigsaw, any day.

Mum was patting her nightgown, rummaging for a tissue. She found one buried in the corner of her pocket, all twisted and used. No wonder. Then she turned to us very seriously indeed and said, 'I never want to hear a mention of this again. If your father ever finds out I've told you, he'll kill me. You have to promise me that you will never mention this to anyone ever again.'

'I promise, Mum.'

'Cross my heart and hope to die.'

'Don't say that. Just promise me.'

'Promise, Mum.'

She floated out into the hallway, lighter than I'd ever seen her before. When she was almost out of sight, she turned back, popped her head across the threshold, 'No more fighting?'

'Yes, Mum.' 'No, Mum.' We both answered at the same time. Ger was as upside down about all this, as I was inside out.

We stood there, staring after her, into the darkness, for ages. Finally we sat ourselves back on to the edge of my bed.

'Sorry, Ger.'

She was rubbing her fingertips along her bruised cheek.

'Does it hurt?'

'What do you think?'

Stupid question. I was hurting all over too.

I rolled back into bed and pulled the pillow over my head. I wasn't bothered about the light.

I said a quiet prayer: 'Dear Jesus, I don't really want to wait for another fifty years to die and go to Heaven, so please take me tonight. I've always wanted to meet you; so why wait?'

I drifted to sleep; down, down, down, into a jelly feeling inside.

All mush and no mould.

When I opened my eyes, the white light in the room nearly blinded me. For a second, I thought I *had* died and gone to Heaven: the silhouette by the window, the flashing lights behind my eyelids . . . Good God, was I finally meeting my Saviour? I panicked. I really wasn't prepared for this. Then, Ger's body slowly emerged from the outline, like Doctor Who's face coming out of the black screen at the beginning of every episode. A Time-Lord from another dimension. She must have spent the night sitting there, on the hearth, at the feet of Jesus, staring ahead, at the faces of Elvis and Neil.

Some Heaven, I thought.

I decided to join her. I knew we had a few problems to solve. Perhaps her Holy Trinity wasn't such a daft idea after all.

I don't know how long we sat there in silence but when I turned to look at Ger, she was beaming at me like a missionary who'd just seen the light. I was really confused. Mum was acting weird, Dad was on a drinking binge, we had a brother we knew nothing about and Ger was grinning at me like a Cheshire cat.

She took me by the hand.

'Don't look at me like that.' I pulled my hand away.

'Seany, we have a brother.'

'We promised.'

'I know but I'm just telling you, nobody else.'

'I don't understand, Ger.'

'You know how Mum's always saying, she wishes she'd finished her nursing training in Liverpool. Well, now we know why she didn't.'

'So?'

'And that night, when Dad was ranting to Mum about choosing which one of us to give away and why my name is "Ger" and you know the way Dad always goes loopy on his birthday?'

'What's there to be so happy about?'

'Things that made no sense, make sense to me now.'

'Maybe, but I'd be a lot happier if things were going to be different from now on.'

'Things will be different. I've decided, Seany, I'm going to run away. I'm going to go to Liverpool and find him.'

'What?'

'It's easy; I'll find Gerald Reilly and bring him back and everything will be different.'

'Mum will kill you.'

'If things stay like this, I'll do it for her.'

I knew what she meant.

'But how will you find him?'

'I have enough information to go on. I know his age, where he was born, his name, all the stuff I need.'

My mind was racing. Ger was going to England to find our brother and I was going to be left on my own, to deal with Dad and Mum. No thanks. Every time Auntie Katie went back home, Mum and Dad would have a massive row. She always insisted on leaving a ton of yellow AA leaflets around the house. Last time, I looked up the words in the dictionary: Alcoholics Anonymous. *Alcoholic*: **1** *adj*. of, pertaining to, or caused by alcohol. **2** *n*. a person addicted to alcoholic drink. *Anonymous*; **1** *adj*. nameless; of unknown name. **2** impersonal, not individuated. I sort of got the gist of it. Anyway, some of the leaflets were right in your face and others, she would hide in funny places like the telephone directory, so they'd drop out for weeks after she'd left. Dad would go mad, tearing them up and ranting about 'his business' and about her 'minding her own business'; then Mum and Dad would row some more. I wasn't looking forward to that, I can tell you.

'I'm coming with you.'

'No, Seany. School starts in three weeks and I won't be back for a while.'

'No way, Ger, I'm not staying here without you.'

'Seany, things will be different when I'm back but it's just not going to work with two.'

'Why?'

'It's easier to hitch a lift with one, easier to find work, easier to eat. All of it; easier.'

'We've got a big match in two days.'

'I'll wait until after the match.'

'No.'

'Look, I won't be going for a week or two, so don't worry, I'll be here when Dad comes back.'

'No, you won't.'

'I will.'

'I don't care. I'm still coming with you.'

'No. It's dangerous and anyway I want you to stay here with Mum.'

She was silent. I could tell she meant it. When she climbed into her bunk and burrowed down like a badger, I knew there was no talking to her. The dawn light was just easing through.

'Good night, John Boy.'

'Good night, Jim Bob', but I lay awake thinking about our trip to England.

Chapter Thirteen

The next day was strange. Mum stayed in bed all day and you'd think relatives were coming home from the States, the way Auntie Katie was up at dawn, cleaning the place from top to bottom, chasing us out from under her feet. On our way to the shop for sweets, Ger gave me the slip when Milo, Joe's younger brother stopped us on his Raleigh bike and told us to choose our favourite colour from a large bag of Opal Fruits. He was only six years old and Mum told us that he'd nearly died when he was a baby from a serious disease called meningitis. On account of that, he didn't have to play sports at school and he had a soft look about him: no chin and watery eyes. Mum said that he was a miracle child; so close to death's door and saved by the angels. He went to Lourdes for blessings every year with his mum and brought back holy water by the gallon. Last summer, Joe and I decided to sell it from a stall just outside their gate. It was cheap if you ask me, two pence for half a yoghurt carton of the Real McCoy. When Milo saw us, he ran at us and kicked the stall over like Jesus in the Temple. Mum said that he had 'priest' written all over him. Personally, I felt sorry for him; everyone deciding what he was going to do before he could even spell his name. Anyway, I looked inside the bag of sweets. Tempting, I can tell you. Ger said, 'What's your problem, Milo? Keep your sweets for yourself.'

He was all wide-eyed and earnest. 'I've bought these with my pocket money and I want to give them away.'

'Why?'

'Have you heard about the parable of the camel and the needle?'

'Yeah.'

'I'm learning to sacrifice everything so I'll have a better chance of getting into Heaven.'

Ger took a green sweet. I, on the other hand, got into one with Milo.

'But Milo, Jesus doesn't mean we have to give everything away.'

'What does He mean then?'

'The parable goes: "It's easier for a camel to pass through the eye of a needle than for a rich man to enter the kingdom of Heaven."'

'Well?'

'It means that it's very difficult for a camel to pass through the eye of a needle but not impossible, it depends how big the needle is.'

'So?'

'The moral of the story is, find a big needle and anything is possible.'

'That's not what my mum says; she says that it's evil to be rich.'

'That's not true. Would you like to own a racing car one day?'

'Yeah.'

'Well, that's not evil. Even Jesus would enjoy a ride in a Ferrari, wouldn't He?'

Ger was tucking in to another green sweet when a gang of lads from Carn Hill Estate crossed over the road to help themselves to Milo's offering. By the time they had cleared off, there was no sign of Ger anywhere.

I shouted at Milo to go home and save up his pocket money for something he really wanted like a football or a kite. That way he could share the fruits of his labour with everyone and have a good time too. He looked after me thoughtfully but no doubt about it, priest was written all over him. Poor sod.

I ran down to the shops to look for Ger. Why do I have to be such an idiot? For a start, if I hadn't been so busy playing Jesus myself, I would still know where Ger was. She could have been anywhere: the bog; the back-fields; the river; Cully's Castle or even down at Mad Tom's orchard. I didn't know where to start, so I went home to pack my suitcase and prepare for the Great Escape.

We didn't say much when she came back for tea. There was a promise hanging between us that we were still not sure how to deal with. I could tell from the smell of her that she'd been messing about in the bog; probably looking for bird's nests in the reeds. I was watching her every move. Ger might have given me the slip today, but she wasn't going to Liverpool, or anywhere else for that matter, without me again.

We went to bed and Mum came to tuck us in.

'Are you all right?' she asked me.

'I'm fine,' I lied.

'Good,' she smiled.

She kissed me on the forehead. I drifted off to sleep wondering why life was like a great big suitcase that never looked any different from the outside: all brown leather, stitching and shiny buckles; but every so often you could open it up, throw in an unusual object, like an iron, or a parrot or a bunch of grapes, and then when you closed it, it looked just the same as before; but you knew, inside, it was all chaos in there.

Anyhow, Mum went back to bed.

The dawn light was just sneaking through when I heard Ger rummaging around in the hot press. She could only be doing one thing, so I shot up, pulled my suitcase from under the bed and stood there ready for action.

'Seany, you're not coming with me.'

'That's what you think. I'm going in to Mum this second to tell her what you're doing if you don't take me.'

'OK, you can come if you promise to do exactly what I say at all times.'

'I promise.'

'OK, you won't be needing this for a start.' I looked down at the small suitcase.

'We'll ride the bikes to Dunford, so we can only take a few things.'

Dunford was about fifteen miles further south, across the border.

'Dunford? You're kidding!'

'Auntie Katie will be home in an hour; she'll sleep until one o'clock. That will give us plenty of time to get there before she notices we're gone.'

She was spitting at me like a sergeant major, so I knew not to argue. She fished in her top drawer, turned and held up a couple of pairs of clean knickers and socks.

I was meant to observe. 'Is that it?'

'Yep. There are some oranges in the bowl downstairs, we'll take them as well.'

'Dunford? OK.'

'Then we get the train to Dublin. Do you have any money?'

I had some pocket money but not much.

'Not enough to get the train.'

'Don't worry about that. We can sneak on to the train and hide in the toilets. I've seen it done loads of times on TV.'

'OK.'

As I got dressed, Ger scribbled a note by the light of the window. Before folding it under her pillow she whispered to me, 'Dear Mum, we've gone to Liverpool to see a man about a dog. Please do not worry about us. We will be back when we have finished our business. We love you. Ger and Seany.' I nodded and followed Ger downstairs into the kitchen, where we filled a white plastic bag with five oranges and our underwear, before slipping out the back door, into the half-light.

We pushed the bicycles along the side of the house, then lifted them over the fence, on account of the creaky gate. We nodded to each other, as if to say 'Let's go' and started riding, up past the Rices', towards the Top road. The place was thick with sleep; the only sound, the wheels whirring on tarmac and the rustle of plastic, as the oranges bobbed about in the bag. We approached Boyle's gate, put on the brakes and stared down the windy, dark road that lay ahead.

'Stick close behind me,' Ger ordered. I glanced back at our house; in the dawn, the face of a ghost, with windows for eyes and a mouth as big as a door calling me home. Ger was already on her saddle and pedalling fast. I'd been down that road more times than I could count but the sight ahead of me was like nothing I'd seen before: rows of overgrown blackberry bushes, dotted through with mountains of red fuchsia and white honeysuckle lining either side, whispering at me through the wind: 'miles to go before I sleep, miles to go before I sleep . . .' I was thinking about Robert Frost and all that 'Stopping By Woods on a Snowy Evening' and then I started wondering why I had to go all stupid like that whenever Ger was furiously cycling through her conscience without a second's thought as to whether 'my little horse must think it queer' . . . I saw the back of her neck: sweat gathering; shoulders hunched over handle-bars and soon I was pedalling close behind gaining speed as we headed towards the Travellers' Crossroads – better to cycle like

179

the clappers than to worry about 'promises to keep' if you want
to make headway through the deep, dark woods . . .

Any time you drove past the Travellers' Crossroads, you never
knew whether the gypsies who'd been there for a week or five
months, would still be there the following day. When they left,
they'd just up and go, silently, leaving long patches of soil to
mark their caravans; like graves, dotted here and there with the
shells of old prams and rusty tyres for headstones. As we
approached I noticed a skinned fox, dangling on the barbed
wire fence. Ger slowed down and I skidded off into the ditch,
knocking the ragged animal to the ground.

'What the Hell, Ger?'

'Shhh.'

She was off her bicycle now, picking her way slowly
towards something in mid-air, with her hands and head jutting
out in front, like a sleepwalker. At first, I couldn't tell what she
was up to, then I saw it too. Hanging there, from one end of a
gatepost on the right arm of the crossroads, then across the
centre to the opposite arm, was a long stretch of tape. It was
tied across the four corners; a frantic black and yellow web,
stopping traffic from every direction. I wheeled my bicycle up
to Ger and we stood staring at it, like it was a puzzle we didn't
know how to solve. We'd seen the tape before when the British
Army cordoned off the area down at Flanagan's shooting. Ger
looked about, but before she even had time to think about
passing underneath, a voice fired at us from the bushes. It was
the unmistakable voice of an English soldier.

'What's in the bag, son?' It was directed at Ger.

We peered behind us in the direction of the sound; then we saw him there, hunched into the bushes in combat gear: the blackened face; the rifle positioned for fire; twigs jutting from his head like a charred pantomime tree. Ger was all eyes.

'What's in the bag, son?' This man wasn't used to asking questions twice.

'Oranges and some knickers.' I leaned across and rustled the bag. The weight around us was so heavy, the song of a sparrow in the hawthorn bush behind pierced through it like a bullet.

When he stood up, he looked slimmer and younger than I expected and the rifle in his hands was almost as tall as he was. He walked up to us, opened the bag and glanced inside.

'You better get off home now.'

'We just want to cycle down to the Dublin road.'

'You better go off home now, you hear.'

'Why can't we go down to the Dublin road?'

My sister was so pushy, I can tell you she'd ask a dead man for directions.

'You better go off home now, before there's any trouble, OK boys.'

He didn't turn his back on us but as he walked away, he looked me in the eye. I stared back at him, wondering what had brought him here, to this crossroads in the middle of nowhere, and I knew that he was wondering the same thing about me. I wanted to tell him about Gerald Reilly, our brother, how we were running away to England to find him but he was already retreating into the shadows. At that moment a shot was fired from somewhere across the fields and he fell to the ground in a heap. He landed face down on an empty caravan patch and I saw his back for the first time. The blood was seeping through his jacket underneath the shoulder-blade.

'Jesus. Let's get out of here.'

Even in a panic, Ger had a plan and I can tell you, the sound of that shot was ringing so loudly in my ears that even if I'd had a better idea, I couldn't have heard it. Before I knew what was happening, we were cycling like crazy, back up the road and away from the bloody scene. I heard an English voice shouting, 'You two boys! Stop!' but we cycled on for dear life. Ger's face was pale and her eyes were red from the effort of cycling through the shock and the nerves. We didn't stop until we reached our house, where we threw the bicycles over the fence and ourselves after them. We bundled them into the coal shed and ran into the kitchen through the back door. When we fell against the door on the inside, we were shaking and panting like two murderers on the run.

Ger turned and grabbed me by both arms. 'It's him, I saw him.'

Her face was so close to mine, I was seeing double.

'What are you talking about?'

'McKee, I saw him, Seany, I saw him, it was him.'

'What are you talking about?'

'Just now. When we were cycling away . . . through Boyle's gate . . . I saw him running through the barley.'

'McKee? How do you know?'

'I saw his red hair, I swear it was him.'

182

'But all that fuchsia, we were going at some speed . . .'

'No, fuchsia doesn't have legs and eyes. It was him, Seany. I swear it.'

'Shit, do you think he was aiming at us?'

'Don't be stupid. If he was aiming at us, he wouldn't have missed.'

My legs gave way from under me and I flopped on to the floor into a small pool of blood that was gathering at my feet. I couldn't see where it was coming from, then I noticed a wet patch on my trouser leg. I touched the spot; my finger pierced the material on my thigh. I pulled the trousers down at the side and there was a gash in my upper thigh where the skin was hanging loose. I must have caught it on the fence on my way over but I still couldn't feel the pain.

'Jesus, it needs a stitch.'

'No way, Seany. We'll have to hold it together with plasters.'

Ger fetched some Dettol and plasters from the medicine cabinet. She cleaned the cut with cotton wool and water. Watching her at work, I felt sad that she wasn't going to be a girl; because the way she unrolled that bandage so neatly around my leg, she would have made a great Florence Nightingale. We tiptoed upstairs and crawled into our beds. For a second, as I lay there, wrapped in the familiar smell of sheets and eiderdowns, it was as if nothing had happened. Then my leg started throbbing under the pressure.

'Ger, what do we do now?'

'We do nothing.'

'But . . .'

'No "buts". We're probably dead meat, Seany, you understand?'

'But we didn't do anything.'

'We were there, that's what we did, and if we're not murdered by our dad, we'll be murdered by Micky McKee and the IRA or by the Brits for getting that soldier killed.'

'But we didn't get him killed.'

'Try explaining that to the RUC or whoever. Don't you see, if we hadn't been there, he'd still be alive.'

'We were just trying to run away, Ger, that's all.'

'Try telling that to Dad and see if you live to tell the tale.'

I could see her point. We were cornered whichever way we turned.

'They torture people for fun, Seany, before they shoot them to death.'

'Who does?'

'Everybody. The Brits, the IRA, the RUC. They all do it.'

'Torture?'

'Branding with hot irons, stabbing, hanging, strangulation, the lot. I don't fancy any of those options, do you?'

'I can't say I do.'

'Well?'

'This is all your fault.'

'Shut up, Seany.'

'Shut up yourself. If you hadn't wanted to be a bloody boy, you'd never have locked Eamo in O'Looney's shed and served Mass that day.'

184

'What are you talking about?'

'That's a mortal sin, I'm sure of it, Ger, and that was the night that Micky McKee nearly shot Dad in the graveyard and then all this.'

'What are you saying?'

'Father Cunningham himself said, "If anyone defiles the temple of God, God will destroy him" and look, look what's happened. We're going to have to emigrate or be tortured to death and it's all because of you.'

'He also said, "Judge not that you be not judged".'

'And a bad workman blames his tools.'

'What's sauce for the goose is sauce for the gander.'

'People in glass houses shouldn't throw stones.'

'A stitch in time saves nine.'

I lay in silence counting the springs on Ger's mattress.

'Ger, I don't want to go to Hell. What's the point of living for years and years if you know you're going to go to Hell at the end of it all?'

'I don't know, Seany. I really don't know. Mum says God is all-forgiving.'

'I'm just not exactly sure what we need to be forgiven for.'

'The gun, the gun by the well. I guess we should have reported it or destroyed it.'

'You don't think . . .'

'I do think.'

'Jesus, did you wipe all the fingerprints off it?'

'I didn't have time.'

The picture was getting muddier and muddier. We were

really in the soup and I could only think of one way to relieve my conscience.

'We have to tell Father Cunningham. Confess. God will forgive us. Father Cunningham can report it to the police without mentioning our names; we're in the clear.'

'Don't be stupid. We have to take this with us to our graves or we'll be hauled up before some tribunal or other. Mum says Father Cunningham has more friends in the IRA than the Pope himself; you don't think they'd let him keep our names out of it?'

'If we can't confess, we'll definitely go to Hell, Ger.'

'We just have to live with that. Maybe if you become a priest it will clear the whole thing up.'

'What about you?'

'I don't know yet.'

Just then we heard the helicopters; steel blades slicing through. We'd seen them land in the back-fields many times before and as I lay there, I could picture what was happening down by the Crossroads: rotors flattening large patches of barley; little green bundles scurrying out and down before diving into the undergrowth for cover.

Next door to the Rices, lived an old man called Brian O'Brien. We'd often send things across to him and one year when dad sent me over with Christmas pudding and beers, O'Brien took out his medals from the Irish Government. He won them for fighting against the treaty in the Old IRA. I asked him what was the difference between the Old IRA and the New IRA and he looked at me in a certain way and I can tell you, he didn't have to say anything for me to know that he thought very little of the

186

new ones. Mum said, she couldn't figure out, why O'Brien didn't live in the Free State that he'd nearly lost his life for; but that day, as he rubbed the medal between his thumb and forefinger, he whispered the words, 'For and against. For and against', like they were a curse, then spoke to me all soft like he was making a confession, 'Son, nothing in this world is worth losing a brother over; *nothing*'. He looked uncomfortable, like he was perched between a rock and a hard place. He told me that he'd fought for a United Ireland and not a half-baked cake, but that he'd rather have no cake at all and a brother to keep him company than a memory, that was sticking in his throat and nearly choking him to death. Mum said, to make matters worse, she'd heard that the brother was *for* the treaty and O'Brien was *against* it. In that case, how in God's name would he know where to live. I guess that was why he lived on the border; a halfway house in the middle of no-man's land. He was as odd as two left feet. Anyway, O'Brien had trained his dogs to bark at the Brits and when they started howling that morning, I knew that the army was pouring silently into the estate like smoke before fire. I went to the window and sure enough, they were filling up the porches, one by one, scouring the place with their guns cocked like oversized toy soldiers.

'Ger, the place is teaming with Brits.'

'Sure it is.'

'There'll be roadblocks all over.'

'I know.'

'Auntie Katie will never get home now.'

'We'll make Mum some breakfast.'

'Is that all you can think of? What if they ransack the house looking for us?'

'They won't ransack the house.'

'Marty Rice says they do it all the time.'

'That's West Belfast. That's the front line, Seany. This is Cherryview Estate. Big difference.'

'I don't know what you're so cocky about. You just said you killed a British soldier and you've got that on your conscience for the rest of your life.'

'*We*, Seany, *we*. You were there too.'

'What do we do now?'

'I keep telling you. We do nothing. They'll be gone soon.'

'My leg's killing me.'

'You're lucky that's all's killing you.'

Ger cleaned the wound and tightened the bandage again, then she made us breakfast. Bacon, eggs and toast is the best cure for what ails you, because as I devoured it watching *Zorro*, I almost forgot about Gerald Reilly and the dead soldier, lying face down at the Travellers' Crossroads.

I had to hand it to her. Ger was right about most things and at the end of *Champion the Wonder Horse*, I looked through the hallway window and there wasn't a soldier in sight. Ger was carrying buttered toast and a cup of hot tea up to Mum. She stopped at the bottom of the stairs, balanced the tray on her knee then tightened her grip on the sides, with her elbows out like a prickly hen. I whispered to her,

'Ger, are you going to mention Gerald Reilly?'

She looked at me as if I was mental.

'Seany, have you ever heard the expression, don't topple the teacup while it's hot?'

'I can't say I have.'

'Well, you have now.'

I was thinking about applecarts or apple tarts as I watched her make her way up the stairs. I bet she didn't spill a drop.

When Auntie Katie came home later, Mum was in the kitchen making soup. She came into the house like a bluster, all shopping bags, coats and talk. I noticed a bundle of AA leaflets on the floor by her nurse's case, so I figured she wouldn't be staying for much longer.

'I was held up with the roadblock. They're stopping and searching every car, I thought I'd never get back.' She turned and glanced at me in the doorway. 'Have you heard the news? A British soldier was shot just down at the crossroads, good God, what next? They're looking for two boys, probably brothers, not older than nine or ten, who were at the scene.' She took out a plastic bag from her right coat pocket, refolded it and placed it back into her left coat pocket. Auntie Katie never threw out anything. Mum said she was blessed because she saw a use for everything in the world. She continued talking with her back to me, 'I mean, what were two young boys doing out at six o'clock in the morning, God only knows.'

As she turned, she noticed Mum and shooed her out of the kitchen like a naughty kitten.

189

'Back to bed, Annie, come on now, I'll bring you up a nice bowl of hot soup.'

In the living room, Ger was watching *The Waltons*. It was one of her favourite programmes so I knew not to say anything but she looked at me,

'Don't say a thing. I heard.'

'I wasn't going to say anything.'

'I said, don't say a thing.'

The red-haired girl, whose name I always forget, was standing in front of a mirror putting apples down her dress, to make her boobies bigger. It was embarrassing; I mean, why rush something that's going to come sooner or later. I glanced across at Ger and I could tell her mind was on other things. She was loose at the seams, like a rag doll who'd been through the hot cycle. It scared the life out of me.

Auntie Katie unpacked the shopping, scattered a few leaflets about and told us that it was time for her to go back home.

'Now, there's steak pie in the fridge. Your mum will be up and about tomorrow.' She must have seen the expression on Ger's face because she softened towards her. 'Now don't you worry, pet, everything will be all right. Your mother just needed a rest and she's better now. OK, you two, be good and I'll see you soon.' Then she must have seen the look on my face because she added, 'Your father, well, he's finally coming round to his senses, thank God', then she blessed herself and rushed out the door.

*

When Dad came home, he was very quiet. He had been to Dunvalley market that morning and he had presents for Ger and me. He placed a huge bunch of flowers against the banisters, then he told us to close our eyes and pick a hand as he held his fists out in front. I pointed to his right hand; he twisted his wrist and gently opened his fingers to reveal a little brass statue of three monkeys. '*Hear no evil; see no evil; speak no evil*', was written underneath and Ger got the same in silver. Watching his clenched fist unfold like a flower as the smile came to the corners of his mouth, sent pins and needles through me. Then he went to the kitchen sink to fill a vase with fresh water. I'd seen a picture of a galaxy, similar to the Milky Way, in one of Ger's library books; it was all splintered lights surrounded in darkness, with a glow in the middle that was so far away, you'd think it was eternity itself. When Dad looked across at me from between the roses, I thought of the Milky Way, all stars and dust cloud, spiralling through the universe and into the black. The sadness floating there went through me so badly, I wished he was drunk so I didn't have to see it.

Mum was up and dressed soon afterwards and we all sat eating Auntie Katie's steak pie with HP Sauce, in front of the six o'clock news. Ger started to choke when they mentioned the dead soldier and gave his name, 'Private James Smith'. What an ordinary name. I imagined myself knocking at the gates of Heaven, asking St Peter to forgive me for my part in the murder of Private James Smith, and Peter would say, 'Which James Smith? We've got ten thousand Privates called James Smith.' Then I'd have to go inside and look at all the faces of all the James Smiths that had died and gone to Heaven and there he would be, staring at me with those eyes and that blood-stained jacket, hunched into a bush, waiting to be identified. I shuddered at the thought, then the newsreader mentioned that two boys, thought to be brothers, had been seen at the scene and the RUC wanted them to come forward. I looked across at Ger; she didn't look like she was having a party either.

That night I slept like a log. I was so tired, if a bomb had gone off, I wouldn't have budged. In the morning I got up and went downstairs before the others. On the coffee table in the living room, one of Auntie Katie's AA leaflets was lying next to the ashtray. The question 'Do You Think You Might Be An Alcoholic?', was at the top of the page and it went on to ask other questions like: 'Have you had problems connected with drinking during the past year?'; 'Has your drinking caused trouble at home?' and 'Have you missed days of work because of drinking?' There were twelve questions and all of them were ticked in the 'Yes' box with red pen. I could tell it was Dad's handwriting: all deep at the start and flick at the end. I heard someone on the stairs and I ran into the kitchen to get some breakfast.

I was about to throw a couple of sausages into the pan, when I turned around; Ger was standing in the hallway facing me. She was dressed in a pink crochet dress that Mum had bought her for Sunday Mass but that she had refused to wear. A pink ribbon tied her fringe back from her face and the buckles on her shiny patent shoes were winking at me in the morning light.

'*Ger?*'

'They're looking for two brothers.'

She was full of surprises, my sister, because if I'd put my money on it, I'd have bet that she would rather have served a jail sentence than give up being a boy but here she was, looking like one of the prettiest girls I'd ever seen, and there was nothing to say except, 'Do you fancy a sausage?' Ger looked a little hurt or something, then I realised what I'd said and I started to laugh. Then Ger started laughing too. Soon we were falling about the place in stitches. My sides were aching so bad, I swear, I thought I was going to burst open from the pain.

Ger carefully cleaned up my leg and we headed off to Mass. No one seemed surprised or shocked at her transition. Marty Rice glanced across during the St Vincent de Paul collection and if anything, he was pleased to see her, all in patent and pink. After Mass, as usual Mrs Sweeney came over to ask after Granny Reilly and Mum and she didn't even bat an eyelid. It was as if Ger had never been a boy. Perhaps this sort of thing happened a lot to girls and the grown-ups just waited patiently for the day when they would come to their senses about not being boys. Complicated.

When we got home, we went upstairs to tidy the bedroom and Ger buried herself in one of her County Library space books. I lay on my bed, gently rubbing the words, '*Hear no evil; see no evil; speak no evil*'. They left a black stain on my fingertips.

'Ger, do you think Dad knows that we know about Micky McKee?'

193

'Listen to this. The universe began with a Big Bang over 10,000 million years ago and it has been expanding outwards ever since.'

'Like a giant bomb?'

'Yeah. It says here that we are all made of stars.'

'Even Micky McKee?'

'Apparently not all stars are the same.'

'Yeah?'

'For example, our sun is a yellow star and there are others that collapse and disappear into the darkness called black holes.'

'Emmm . . .'

'It says here that black holes lock themselves into a dark prison where nothing, not even light, can escape.'

'Is it evil to want someone to be a black hole?'

'Not if they are one already.'

'What happens to them?'

'They suck in everything around them and then they die.'

'What sort of star is Gerald Reilly?'

'A shooting star, Seany, he's a shooting star.'

'I love shooting stars.'

'Me too.'

'What are they?'

'Meteors.'

'That's nice.'

'It says here, "When the earth moves around the sun, it collides with small particles of rocks that heat up, burn then shoot through the atmosphere."'

'I guess there are millions of them out there.'

'Millions. Sometimes there are meteor showers.'

'What's that?'

'When we pass through a really rough patch, like a comet, and the earth hits more rocks than usual.'

'I think we've been through one of those lately.'

'Yeah.'

The following day, there was a football match on the Green. While I cleaned my boots on the back step, Ger was busy in the coal shed working on her Apollo 11 spacecraft. She was standing on Mum's stepladder, sticking tin foil on to a cardboard flap and applying the final heat shield. I watched her for a minute and then headed up to the Green.

After tea, Dad switched on the news. Riots had broken out in West Belfast and there was no mention of Private James Smith and the two brothers down at the Travellers' Crossroads. Dad was taking Mum out for a meal to the Forest House Hotel, just outside Dunvalley town and Mags, our 'baby-sitter', was coming round at about seven o'clock. After the news, I tried to get a minute with Ger to talk about Ginger McKee. If he was a black hole, from what I understood, anything that falls into one can never get out and I could still feel the suction dragging me down. I made a few signals to Ger to get her attention and went upstairs, expecting her to follow me up. I hopped on to Ger's bunk and was about to take McKee's photo out from under her pillow when I heard the counting. As loud and as clear as if I was doing it myself, Marty Rice was doing keepie-uppie outside on the footpath below the open bedroom window.

'Forty-four, forty-five, forty-six . . .'

No doubt he could afford to show off.

I heard a movement on the landing. From the top bunk, I could see over the doorway. Ger was standing with her back to me, looking through into Mum's bedroom. Mum was sitting at the dressing table in her underwear, carefully applying her eyelashes. When they were in place, she blinked at herself like a woman who'd just got new eyes and was testing them out for size; then she reached for her lipstick, stretched her lips around her mouth like a big cat's meow, hiding her teeth then showing them again, as she applied it and tidied up the edges with her painted fingertips. Her hair fell about her face in soft curls and as she reached for the green necklace that hung over the side of the mirror, I saw just how beautiful she was.

'Sixty, sixty-one, sixty-two, sixty-three.'

The doorbell rang and Ger jumped as Mum shouted through:

'Go get it, Ger. That'll be Mags.'

She turned quickly, bumping into me, and threw me a disgusted look.

'What did I do?'

'You shouldn't sneak up on a person like that.'

'You were sneaking up on Mum.'

'I was not.'

'You were.'

'Was not.'

'What's the matter with you two?' Mum asked.

She didn't expect an answer. She was looking at us through the mirror. It was like having two mums. The one facing us, with a smile like a sea breeze, warm one minute, cool the next, and the other, with her back to us, all skin and bone from the effort of stretching forwards into the light. Ger pushed past me and stomped down the stairs.

'I want no nonsense from either of you when Mags is here. Supper at eight, bed at nine, OK?' Mum was at the door already.

'OK,' I said and she smiled at me as she closed it over gently.

Not long after Mum and Dad left, I was watching TV with Mags.

'Fifteen, sixteen, seventeen . . .' He must have dropped the ball and started counting again. It was getting dark, so I got up to close the window and draw the curtains when I saw a figure moving out of the light. Ger glanced back at me; I could just make out her lips and eyelids – red and green with no amber in between. She turned away, raised her arms, whipped herself over on to her hands, legs following through into the air; all knickers, buckles and eyes, flashing into the darkness, as she cartwheeled across the grass like a spiral galaxy. Marty Rice looked up at her from the footpath by the fence. He didn't even go after the ball as it rolled away. She stood there in the middle of the garden, her hair all ruffled, like one of the dancers in an Elvis movie.

'Do you want to see my Apollo spacecraft?'

If a girl ever asked me a question like that, I'd be surprised, but he answered 'Sure', as if he was asked to see a spacecraft every day of the week. He hopped over the fence like the Bionic Man and followed Ger into the coal shed.

Mags lit up a cigarette and asked me not to tell Mum or Dad. I said no problem. I went into the kitchen to fix myself some supper and a chill was blowing through the open door. I followed it out into the garden and from the shadows by the hedge, I could see into the shed. Ger's circuit board sparkled against the silver foil, then I saw them leaning against the bicycles, all sprinkled in coloured lights like a human Christmas tree. They were stumbling between the pedals and the handlebars, kissing and gasping for air. Suddenly, Ger pulled away and reached for a book from inside the command module. It was the one she'd shown me earlier, called *Space and the Universe*. I quickly disappeared around the side of the shed and into the gooseberry patch. They sat on the step, looking at the shiny pictures. He kept slipping his arm around her shoulder but she shimmied it away. Girls are strange. I don't think I'd want to be one for all the whiskey in Ireland.

They were looking at a picture of Neil Armstrong walking on the moon.

'Isn't it amazing?' Ger said.

'Not as amazing as this,' and he tilted Ger's head upwards to look at the sky. It was a clear night and the three of us looked up in awe at the clusters of twinkling stars, stretching out like a magic carpet, splintering into smithereens above us.

'There's one,' Ger could hardly speak as she pointed at a meteor falling away into the distance.

'You get to make a wish.'

Ger was silent and I could tell she was thinking of *him*. Whether Mum and Dad knew it or not, Gerald Reilly was lighting up the darkness all around us.

'Look, there's another one.' He was as excited as she was.

I held up my hand to try and catch it as it fell through my fingers, glowing and trailing into the air, out of my reach.

*

For days afterwards, I tried to talk to Ger about Micky McKee but she said that she had other things on her mind. Mum said she thought it was time for Ger to have her own room and she asked Dad if he would clear out the boxroom for me. As soon as Dad was out of the house, I placed the 1971 school album, with McKee's picture, back on to the shelf where we'd found it. It was as if it had never been moved.

On the following Thursday, the story was on the front page of the *Dunvalley Reporter*. There was a photo of the dead soldier and a mention of the two brothers at the scene of the shooting. Ger was biting her fingernails. I could tell from looking that she was still as scared as I was. She disappeared up to our room and I walked in, just as she was removing the monkey statues from the mantelpiece.

'What are you doing?'

'All those eyes . . .' She folded them in a pillowcase and hid them in the hot press.

Hear no evil; see no evil; speak no evil; buried beneath blankets in our very own bedroom.

'That won't get rid of the problem,' I said.

'I think we should meet with McKee.'

'What are you on about?'

'We should meet with him and make a deal.'

'What sort of deal?'

'Tell him that we know everything and we won't go to the police if he swears on his mother's life to leave us all alone.'

'What if she's dead?'

'OK, on his mother's grave then.'

'We can't do that.'

I'd made that mistake once and once was enough to know that it wasn't a wise beginning to any deal. Those words: 'My mother's dead'; they just wipe the carpet right from under your feet and you end up feeling sorry for them and getting punched in the head as well. Not good.

'OK, we just get him to swear on his life.'

'Jesus.'

'What choice do we have? I can't go on like this, Seany, I can't do it. Otherwise we go to the police and get him arrested, just to get him out of our hair but we'll definitely have to request protective custody.'

'What's that?'

'Marty Rice told me, it's when you get a new name and move to Canada or Australia and start all over again.'

'Become a grass, you mean.'

'No, we're not doing that, we're going to strike a deal with him, idiot.'

*

So that was it. Mum was going to Dunvalley town on Thursday morning and we asked her to drop us off at the swimming pool while she did the shopping. The swimming pool was at the bottom of the Loughlow road, a long hill that led out of Dunvalley and up to Stonecroft Estate. Stonecroft Estate was hard-man territory. Once, after Bloody Sunday, the whole place was green, white and gold flags, lamp-posts and paving stones; a fairground with no rides or toffee-apples. The estate was surrounded by a tall stone wall that circled the houses, held them tightly in. Driving by, from the hill, it looked like one of those round cake tins with the mix all sizzling around the sides, under the heat of a hot oven. Stick a knife in and if it comes out clean, it's well cooked.

One evening, on the way to Granny Reilly's, a trail of British Army tanks and RUC armoured vehicles was driving through the gates to the housing estate. A dozen or so soldiers rushed out, and surrounded a house. As they were kicking the door down, we drove under the arches, out of sight, and I had to imagine the rest. The estate was so out of bounds that Mum had never even mentioned to us not to go there.

As Mum pulled away in the car, Ger and I made our way to the swimming-pool entrance. We waved at her; went in one door; waited, and came out the other. I was about to head straight back through the swing door again: a circle is an intelligent way out of a straight line, especially if it's a straight line that's leading to no good. But Ger grabbed my elbow and we turned left, as planned, and headed up the hill towards Stonecroft.

The deceit was playing havoc with my insides. It was as if I'd swallowed a mountain of bubble gum, and someone was crawling around my guts blowing a bubble so large, it was sending me up, up, up and away from all I knew and trusted. My jumper was tightening around my throat and every step I took away from the truth of where we were meant to be, was shooting pins and needles straight through me; if only they'd burst the bubble. I'd heard the expression used when people were so excited about something that they were living in cloud-cuckoo-land and had to come down to earth with a bang. Like the time Mrs O'Rourke from our estate won the pools but she forgot to tell the organisers that her sister had helped her to pick the numbers. Mum read out the article in the *Reporter*; it said that 'Mrs O'Rourke insisted that the sister was only in the same room as herself and hadn't helped her at all'. They had to spend all the money on a court case that went on for years and Mum said that the whole nonsense 'fairly burst their bubble'. On my way up the hill, I wasn't excited, I was nervous as hell but I couldn't help thinking that if I'd won the pools, I'd have handed the lot over to the first person who showed up to burst my bubble. I felt so high, I was sure I was floating ten feet off the ground; McKee would take one look at me and drop dead with fright, thinking an angel of the Lord had appeared to ask him to mend his wicked ways.

'Why don't we go back and swim like we said we would?'

'If we don't do this we'll be swimming all right; up to our necks for the rest of our lives, Seany.'

My sister had a way with words. I knew we were up to our

necks in it already and it looked like there was only one way out.

When there's only one way out, you know you're in big trouble. In early summer, the honeybees foraged around the bushes that sprouted their yellow flowers, up on Cherryview Lawns. Watching them busily collecting nectar and pollen welled something up in me that made me want to snatch them into jam-jars and screw the lid on tight. Yes, I would get a good look at the thin wings and the furry bodies but a small, sharp pleasure came from watching their frustration as they buzzed against the glass, longing for the sweet flowers outside. For seconds, I couldn't decide whether to open the lid or watch them slowly die, cooking on the palm of my hand, in the warm sun. I called the game Fly or Fry. Once I plucked a daisy and asked the petals, 'Fly or fry?' That summer, I had the beginnings of a cruel streak in me; I wasn't pleased about it but I was so relieved when the final petal said, 'Fly' that I reckoned my cruel streak was only there to show me just how close my good streak was. I mean, no matter what, sooner or later I always twisted off the lid in time. *Only one way out*; usually if there's only one way out, someone else knows about it too and that person is someone you'd rather not know about it at all: McKee. He was probably waiting for us to show up: like two honeybees caught in jam-jars with the lids tightly twisted and no holes for air.

When we got close to the Stonecroft entrance, we were hit by the screams of swarming kids. We walked past the painted stones, all 'Up the "Ra"' and 'Provos Rule', and saw into the heat. About thirty boys and girls were running after a boy: Rope Tig. So, they had their Marty Rices too; wee lads who lived in West Belfast and who came to Stonecroft for their summer holidays with games and stories that made them feel, no matter what happened on their estate, it would never be as hard or as dangerous as what happened on the front line.

We stood there watching as the boy was caught and wrapped around with rope like a loin of cooked pork. We weren't in the mix yet and I was thinking, it wasn't too late to turn back when a boy, ginger-haired, big ears and a grin so wide you could drive a train through it, turned and stared. He was a mini-McKee.

'My God, it's him,' I whispered to Ger. 'He's the same age as us.'

'Don't be daft, it's his brother.'

The mass of faces turned towards us and I saw another five McKees, from ages seven up to fourteen, their caps of wild ginger hair dotted through the crowd of dark heads like a cluster of scarlet toadstools. I remember Dad warning us about toadstools. 'Pay close attention to the characteristics,' he said, 'including the appearance and the smell of the cut flesh. A mistake could prove fatal.' Mum came out to the yard and saw him lining up all the different types that were growing in Granny Reilly's back-field and she flared into a row with him for encouraging us to touch them at all. He got into one with her about how we needed to know one from another but the whole thing got spoiled so even if Dad had gone back to explaining, I wouldn't have wanted to remember what he'd said. Well, right now, I wished Mum had just stayed inside and let him get on with it because I wanted to know whether the species facing us was about to prove fatal.

'You two, where you from?' the boy shouted across to us and you could tell from his mouth and the way his teeth chewed on the corner of his lower lip after he spoke, that he wasn't afraid of anything.

'Well . . .' I started. I had no idea what I was going to say. I was probably going to come out with something about bees and floating bubbles.

'We're just waiting on our auntie,' Ger said.

'Who's that?'

'Auntie Katie. The nurse, she's doing her dressings and diabetics. She told us to wait by the gate. Can we play?'

They looked round at each other and the boy, the tallest ginger one, nodded.

'Sure. OK, everyone, two teams for football.'

Jesus. We were in the soup now. How were we going to get out of a game of footie in time to get hold of Micky McKee, make a deal and get out alive?

The best thing about kids, I swear, is once you're in you're in. I mean, after he'd nodded at us, we might as well have lived across the road from the McKees the way we were included in the game.

A few of the girls dwindled off and soon we were stuck into a decent game. I was on the opposite team to Ger and when she came in for a tackle, I fouled her real bad just to show the

205

others that we weren't up to anything suspicious. 'Strategy,' I whispered to her when I helped her on to her feet. She glared at me but I knew what I was doing. After about ten minutes, Micky McKee walked straight down from the houses towards the Green. There he was, a mountain of a man, about six feet tall and the spit of the photo in the school album. I was approaching the box, set for a goal when I looked up and saw him walking towards us as cocky as someone who'd just bought new shoes. I lost control of the ball and kicked it high and wide. He ran after it laughing, 'What's with the banana boots?'

'That's the nurse's nephew, he's OK,' said mini-McKee.

McKee dribbled the ball back down the footpath and rushed on to the pitch with as much skill and style as Georgie Best himself. From the way all the lads ran after him, you could tell he did this a lot: hijacked the game just to show off and everyone else enjoyed it too. He was awesome. As he dribbled the ball from one end of the pitch to the other he nutmegged every pair of legs until he came to Ger's. She was standing staring at him in disbelief when he chipped the ball cheekily over her head and ran around her in time to volley it with the outside of his foot past the goalie. It hit the wall, so close to the top, I thought it would burst on the broken glass that stuck up like coloured lights around the edge but it bounced back with such force that the goalkeeper dived to miss it. McKee ran after the ball and was doing the fanciest keepie-uppies I'd ever seen: toe to knee to head to neck to toe and that's when all the lads just stopped and stared too. I'd never seen anyone do what he could do with a ball. McKee looked up at the faces, laughed and started dribbling the ball back down the pitch, his jacket flapping open, with his arms up in the air, like a great big bird, cheering himself on, like he'd just scored for Ireland. I'll say one thing: photographs don't show how much life there is in a pair of eyes because it looked like two stars were shining there, with more going on behind them than I'd ever seen in a living soul. His eyes were laughing eyes, they really were. Laughing eyes.

As Micky made his way down the pitch, the other McKees started to jump on to his back, trying to wrestle him to the ground. 'Sweets! Sweets!' they were chanting and he tumbled to the ground with a face and eyes so excited, you couldn't even imagine him hurting a fly. He disappeared beneath a pile of arms and legs and I could just make out his lanky fingers rustling in his pocket. He tore out a bag of cola cubes and held them high, asking for mercy as he crawled out from beneath the scrum. He had a beard; that was the only difference from the photo, and as he handed the sweets out one by one, it made him look more like Jesus with the loaves and fishes, than you'd care to believe. Then from between the goals, at the other end of the pitch, a little girl, she must have been four, all red hair and freckles, started running towards him, shouting his name: 'Micky, Micky.' He handed the bag to a mini-McKee and he ran towards her, arms outstretched, and lifted her up like a doll, throwing her into the air. I stood there watching and wishing that someone, anyone, would run towards me and throw me up like that, then I looked back at Ger; she was standing speechless too.

I started to retch.

Ger ran up to me.

'Quick, let's get out of here.'

'But that's him, we've come all this way, let's nail him.'

'It can't be. There's no way that's him, Seany.'

'Jesus.'

And we took our chance; they swarmed around the bag of sweets and we ran. At the gates, Ger took one look back at McKee. I could see a longing inside her, too. He couldn't have been more than eighteen. An older brother to die for. Perhaps Gerald Reilly was an older brother to die for too.

'Come on, run,' she said and we legged it back down the hill to the entrance to the swimming pool. We sat on the wall outside the pool to catch our breath.

'Ger, what do we do now?'

'I don't know, Seany. But one thing I know is, it isn't him, no way.'

'Looks like we're back to square one.'

'We'll have to go to Father Cunningham, tell him everything.'

'Even about Eamo and the altar wine?'

'That too. It's our last chance. Ask for forgiveness and leave it in the hands of the Lord.'

'Do you think that's wise?'

'Not really, but it's the only way out for us now.'

'Do you think Dad made a mistake too?'

'Yeah I do, I really do. It could be another Micky McKee but it's not that one, that's for sure.'

A haze of colour burst behind my eyes: yellow flowers,

distorting and magnifying through glass. I thought I was going to faint.

The real McKee was out there and we had no idea who he was or where to find him. I dropped my head between my legs to catch my breath. Ger put her hand on my back.

'You all right?'

I nodded.

'I know what you mean, Ger, he's far too good at football to be a gunrunner.'

'It's not that,' said Ger. 'If I had an older brother like him, I probably wouldn't ever have wanted to be a boy.'

We sat in silence. I wasn't sure what she meant.

'Ger?'

'Don't get me wrong, Seany, you're a great brother, the best, but imagine having someone like that on our side, big and funny and great. Dad would never fight with Mum again.'

We were so wet with sweat, we didn't have to pour water on our heads to make it look like we'd been swimming.

'Let's go inside and soak our towels.'

'Yeah,' she said, 'let's soak our towels.'

That evening, Ger was sitting on the edge of the hearth in her pyjamas, staring at the poster of Neil Armstrong landing safely on the Sea of Tranquillity. It was beyond me to guess what was going through her mind. She hadn't even noticed me standing there, watching, so I left her quietly, lost in space.

*

As swiftly as a broom clears feet from the hallway, the summer holidays were swept aside and it was time to get ready for the new term. One day it was all loose ends and football and the next it was a rush of new books, new shoes, new haircuts and new resolutions. It was better than confession or New Year's Eve for making me feel like a soul with every possible hope of redemption. Mum took Ger into town for a school uniform and I wasn't allowed into Murphy's – The One-Stop Shop for Ladies. It had things in the window that made you want to stare at the pavement as you walked by: ladies' pants and mannequins dressed in large girdles, as well as cushions and curtains and sewing machines. The mind boggled. In September, Ger was starting at the grammar school for young ladies on Wicklow Street and she would have to wear a pleated skirt and a shirt that showed the bra-strap through the back in summer. I'd seen those on grammar-school girls buying chocolate éclairs and meringues in the Star Bakery before. I was really tempted to twang one, just once, to see if I could catapult someone straight into a sherry trifle.

After the hush and rustle of bags in and out of the boot of the car, I could tell that Mum had bought Ger a bra. When we got home, she disappeared upstairs and into the bathroom with a brown bag tucked under her arm. I had only just plonked on to the sofa to watch TV when a newsflash interrupted the weather report. A young man, identified as Michael McKee, had died in an explosion at his home in Stonecroft Estate, Dunvalley; he had been assembling an incendiary device in his attic when the explosion suddenly went off. They showed a picture of his face.

It was the same as the one in Dad's album. Like I said, that photo didn't show the light in his eyes but it was him all right; he was 'Ginger-the-Killer' after all. I started chewing the skin around my thumb, I drew blood, the pain shot along my hand and as I shook it away, I bolted up the stairs and into the bathroom to tell Ger. She was brushing her teeth in the mirror and she dropped her head into the sink and burst into tears.

'What's wrong, Ger?'

She sat on the edge of the bath, all crumpled inwards like an injured bird and I could see the strap; there it was, a small ridge across the middle of her back, branding her with a stroke of luck that somehow drew a line under things for the both of us.

I pulled off a piece of toilet roll and handed it to her.

'God forgive me but I'm glad,' she said.

'I know,' I said.

'And sad.'

I knew what she meant.

A waste of everything, that's all I could think of; a waste.

'Do you think we still have to go to confession?'

Ger looked up at me and I'll never forget it.

She said, 'I don't know any more if we are to blame for anything we do.'

'What do you mean?'

'If you look at it differently, it's hard to know whose fault it is, or when it all started.'

'You've changed your tune.'

'Well, I asked Neil Armstrong what he thought about it all.'

'And what did he say?'

'He said that when he saw the earth from the moon for the first time, *everything* was changed in an instant.'

'I see.'

'*In an instant*, he realised that what he thought about something, depended on which angle he was looking at it from and he added – the more he finds out, the less he knows.'

'Just like us?'

She nodded.

'Did Elvis say anything?'

She nodded again.

'He said he's all shook up too.'

'Just like us?'

She smiled at me from that place behind the eyes, where there is no beginning and no ending.

'Ger, do you know, you are one of the people who the wind blows through.'

'I'm hurting, Ger.'

'Just think of it as love, turned inside out.'

'When will it turn outside in?'

'I guess, when we see it from the stars.'

'What if I can't reach that far?'

'You have already.'

She moved towards me and pulled me to her. As we stood there, hugging tightly, the smell of bacon and eggs filtered up the stairs and I felt the universe expanding outwards and spiralling towards forever.

WEDNESDAY'S CHILD

Eloise Millar

'Dick Roberts didn't belong in the kitchen, even at the best of times. It was Mum and Nan's, not his. When he was there he seemed to lurk in it, like a furtive hyena on the periphery of a lion's den . . . Talk died whenever he entered the room, and half-finished conversations hung subversively in the air, mingling with the cigarette fog.'

Janet Roberts and her brother James are at the mercy of their father's foul mood swings, especially on Wednesdays, when he returns from his third nightshift of the week, angry and red-eyed, looking for trouble. But they can always lose themselves in Janet's stories of ghosts and gypsies, or go and visit their boozy Aunt Net, who welcomes them with open arms as long as they make a visit to the off-licence first.

Then, in the course of one summer on their Oxford council estate, everything changes. A young girl is found murdered in the park near their house. James disappears, Aunt Net goes off the rails and Janet's mother is hospitalised. Janet is left to fight her battles alone, with only her quick wits and vivid imagination to help her through.

In this affecting and spirited novel, Eloise Millar brings to life a community, a family and a valiant, lovable heroine. *Wednesday's Child* is a remarkable and original debut from an exciting new voice in fiction.

'Millar creates a child's all-seeing, all-accepting world view . . . and brings vividly before you the lives of people who have lost the will to change' *The Times*

AN EMPTY ROOM
Talitha Stevenson

After months away, Emily returns to London and to a family on the verge of disintegration. She spends nights in cramped bars, drinking and smoking with her beautiful but damaged boyfriend Tom and his friends.

It is a lifestyle that leaves her feeling directionless and jaded. In her search to believe in something or someone, she finds herself irresistibly drawn to Simon, Tom's complex and charming cousin. But Simon is married, and as he and Emily become closer and the summer draws to an end they are forced to make decisions that will have a devastating effect on both families.

'So lucent, so resonant, so exquisitely written and above all, so engaging' Tim Lott, *Evening Standard*

'Its denouement ought to surprise none but Emily herself, cast adrift in her own love stories, yet *An Empty Room* echoes with the dreamy unreality of a hot summer night' *Observer*

'A stunning debut . . . an exquisite, stylishly written novel' *Irish Examiner*

'Set in a coolly evoked city landscape, *An Empty Room* perfectly encapsulates the confusions and mistakes of a young adult and tells us something significant about the furies and hurts of first love' Elizabeth Buchan

Now you can order superb titles directly from Virago

☐ Wednesday's Child	Eloise Millar	£6.99
☐ An Empty Room	Talitha Stevenson	£6.99
☐ State of Happiness	Stella Duffy	£6.99

The prices shown above are correct at time of going to press. However, the publishers reserve the right to increase prices on covers from those previously advertised, without further notice.

Virago

Please allow for postage and packing: **Free UK delivery.**
Europe: add 25% of retail price; Rest of World: 45% of retail price.

To order any of the above or any other Virago titles, please call our credit card orderline or fill in this coupon and send/fax it to:

Virago, PO Box 121, Kettering, Northants NN14 4ZQ
Fax: 01832 733076   Tel: 01832 737526
Email: aspenhouse@FSBDial.co.uk

☐ I enclose a UK bank cheque made payable to Virago for £ . . . .
☐ Please charge £ . . . . . . to my Visa/Access/Mastercard/Eurocard

☐☐☐☐☐☐☐☐☐☐☐☐☐☐☐☐☐☐

Expiry Date ☐☐☐☐   Switch Issue No. ☐☐

NAME (BLOCK LETTERS please) . . . .

ADDRESS . . . .

. . . .

. . . .

Postcode . . . . Telephone . . . .

Signature . . . .

Please allow 28 days for delivery within the UK. Offer subject to price and availability.

Please do not send any further mailings from companies carefully selected by Virago ☐